WINTER KILLS

A Victor Storm Novella

TERRY F. TORREY

Visit terryftorrey.com for a complete list of works by Terry F. Torrey, and subscribe to the newsletter to be notified of promotions, special events, and new releases of things worth reading.

This is a work of fiction. All of the characters, organizations, and events portrayed in this work are ether products of the author's imagination or are used fictitiously.

Copyright © 2007 by Terry F. Torrey. All rights reserved.

2024-01-09

For Ceyshé

CHAPTER ONE

In the dream, he's walking through the north St. Louis neighborhood on his way home from school. It's a late autumn day, and the sky is crystal blue above. The weather has been brisk and snappy, but this afternoon summer seems to have breathed one last warm gasp into the city. He's smiling. He wears a jacket, but it's warm, and he is thinking about taking it off and carrying it. He walks alone. The leaves crackle underfoot.

He is happy today, contented. For the first time since his family moved here, he feels at home. He has finally adjusted to his new junior high. He has found some good people, some of whom have become his friends, and he has identified some bad people, all of whom are to be avoided. He is finally beginning to know his place in the school, the city, and even the world.

Up ahead, the far corner of the line of trim red brick townhouses where he lives has just come into view when he hears a strange whistle of wind, then a thumping roll in the grass off to his right. Catching a glimpse out of the corner of his eye, he at first thinks it is a baseball, and he smiles. The smile leaves his face when he realizes that it is a rock thrown from behind him.

Ducking just a bit reflexively, he turns back to see a group of three boys behind him a ways across the street. He did not want to see these boys. They are not his friends. They are people to avoid.

Before he has time to react, there's a whirl of an arm, and a tiny arc of gray motion, and a rock hits him just above his right eye.

He reels sideways from the blow, almost falling down in the street. Another rock snaps off the asphalt and cracks against the curb. His head suddenly feels large and heavy. His feet chase slowly under his tipping body before he gets his balance. His eyebrow feels wet.

And then he is running. Another rock swishes through the air past his ear as he reaches the sidewalk. He makes the split-second decision to dodge between the houses to his right rather than run straight up the street, where he would be an easy target.

He picks up speed, dashing down the driveway toward the narrow gap between the garage and the house next door. A rock clacks off the picket fence out front.

Suddenly, his path is blocked. Someone has put up a new redwood fence from the garage to the house, closing in the backyard but shutting him out. The fence is tall—too tall to jump over, too tall to climb over quickly. He can hear footsteps running through the leaves behind him. His mind in a panic, he ducks through the side door into the garage. As he reaches for the door, he can see a spot of blood on the web of his hand between his thumb and forefinger.

All at once, he isn't twelve anymore; he's twenty-nine. He isn't alone; he's with his team. He isn't in a darkened garage; he's in a house in a suburb of Baghdad.

It's chilly outside, but it's hot under his bulletproof vest, and he's thinking about taking it off.

Suddenly, an Iraqi man walks in and spots him. His rifle swings up. The man's mouth opens.

It isn't a warm fall day in St. Louis. It's Christmas Eve in Iraq.

In his bed, he's drenched in sweat, and he tries desperately to wake from the dream.

In his apartment in downtown St. Louis, Victor Storm woke with a start, gulping breath, heart pounding. He drew his hands up in front of his face, expecting to look at the rifle he was holding, but as his eyes adjusted, he saw they were empty.

The studio apartment materialized from the darkness around him. A rectangle of soft, gray light entered the room from around the blinds closed across his front window. His eyes searched the darkness, finding reassurance in the familiar forms of the lamp on the nightstand next to his queen bed, the wide, low bookshelf between his bed and the living area, the arch to the kitchen, and the kitchen counter. His ears picked up the distant rumble of a diesel engine idling somewhere in the parking lot outside, and this, too, was familiar and reassuring.

For a while, he sat on the edge of the bed. Though it was still before dawn, he didn't want to go back to sleep.

In time, he walked to the window, twisted the blinds open, and stared out at the darkness. His apartment was too low to the ground and too far away, but he could imagine he could see the flat black Mississippi River rolling through the darkness. He could almost see the Arch, rising and falling like hope, like life.

In the eastern distance, he could see the first touch of blue beginning to lighten the far horizon.

CHAPTER TWO

As soon as Victor Storm walked into the philosophy class at St. Louis Community College, he thought he had made a mistake.

A number of things had led him here. He'd never been to college before. He'd joined the Army right out of high school. After twenty years, he was thirty-eight and retired. Wow. A year later, his wife left him, and a year after that he turned forty. In the year and a half since then, he'd been trying to sort out the big issues of life, the universe, and everything. He'd looked in a lot of bars, but he hadn't found any answers, or insight, or anything but drunks and thugs.

Then, skimming through his junk mail one day, he'd come across a flyer for the St. Louis Community College. His eyes fell on the description of a philosophy class: "An introduction to philosophical inquiry through a study of such perennial problems as the nature of truth and the possibility of knowledge, the various conceptions of the mind-body relation; the nature and basis of morality; the problem of free will and an analysis of the main arguments for the nature and existence of God." Wow.

Reading this, the wheels in his head had begun to turn.

He'd become more introspective in recent years. His early retirement, and his wife's leaving him and taking their daughters back to her family in North Carolina, had left him with a lot of free time and a lot of uncertainty. Now that he could do what he wanted, he had no idea what might be the right thing to do. He had found himself up against the big questions of life: Who am I? Why am I here? What should I do with my life? And, turning the questions over in his head, he had found himself not just without answers, but without an idea of how to figure out the answers. He'd been absolutely and totally lost. Seeing the flyer for the community college class, he'd felt the tiniest flicker of hope in his heart. Maybe, just maybe, a philosophy class would help him to sort things out. He had decided to give it a shot. Even if it didn't give him the answers, it could possibly introduce him to a framework of thinking about things to let him work out the answers for himself.

He had hoped that by taking an evening class that he would perhaps have the company of some other people his own age, and that maybe he would find some other people with similar issues, similar problems, solutions he hadn't been able to think of on his own. Looking around the class now, Victor began to doubt the whole enterprise.

He saw he was by far the oldest one there. At ten minutes early, he had been the first one to arrive, and he'd been able to watch his "classmates" arrive. By ones and twos, they straggled in, took seats, and began talking about non-issues as if they were important. All of them were kids, none of them older than their early twenties.

When the "instructor" came in and took a seat at the desk up front, Victor's dismay was complete. This guy was barely older than most of the students. What could he possibly know? The drunks down at Penguin's Tavern probably knew more than this guy; they'd certainly seen more of life. If Victor had been seated near the door, he might have left, but he was in the far back corner of the room, so he merely sat there and thought about it.

The instructor glanced at the clock, then cleared his throat to get the attention of the class. "Okay, everyone. This is Introduction to Philosophy, so if you were looking for something else, this would be an excellent time to leave."

A general chuckle rose up from the class. No one left, though Victor thought very seriously about it.

"My name is Colton Fischer," the instructor continued, "and as you have probably figured out, I'm the instructor for this class. This will be a survey of philosophy, in which we talk about things like metaphysics, epistemology, ethics, aesthetics, and logic."

"What about truth?" someone in the middle of the room suggested.

Colton Fischer smiled. "That's a good question."

Again, a little laugh rose up from the room.

"Yes," Colton Fischer continued, "truth, knowledge, free will, existence, ethics, beauty—we'll get to all of that in time. First, though, I'm supposed to start with something a little less heady: a roll call."

This introduction actually made Victor feel a little better. Truth, free will, ethics—even if nobody here had any real insight into the answers of the world, maybe he could learn something just by hearing the questions.

While Colton Fischer—Victor refused to think of him as "Mr." Fischer—called names off his roster, Victor watched the students, trying to remember names and generally occupying himself by observing the students. The skill of observation was highly prized in the Special Forces, and Victor was good at it.

Colton Fischer finished his roll call, then stood up and leaned on his desk. His face showed the expression of a man formulating a thought. "How many people are taking this class because it's required for a degree?" he asked.

Half or more of the hands went up.

"And people taking it because they have a real interest in philosophy?"

A few of the remaining hands went up. Victor saw Colton Fischer sneak a glance at him each time, though Victor didn't raise a hand for either answer.

"I think that's a good mix," Colton Fischer continued. "I've found that people taking the class because they *have* to feel free to argue whatever points they like, while people taking the class because they *want* to really try to apply the concepts we talk about, and provide a kind of structure to the debate." He walked over to the blackboard and picked up a piece of chalk. "Now, before we begin, I'd like to make a list of the kinds of questions and concepts that people think of when they think about philosophy." He looked back over his shoulder at the class, hand poised to write on the board. "Anybody? Philosophical question or concept?"

"Uhm," said a guy in the other back corner of the room, "boxers or briefs?"

Everyone but Victor laughed. Colton Fischer wrote it on the board.

"Abortion?"

Colton wrote it on the board.

"Racism."

On the board.

The death penalty, war, the legal system—all on the board.

After the board was sufficiently scratched with questions and terms, Colton began to address the points, commenting on how different philosophical concepts addressed the various issues, and how their studies during the course of the semester would give them a framework for thinking about these things.

During Colton's lecture, he posed questions to the group, solicited answers, then posed more questions about those answers. Some of the students were more willing than others to speak up, but all of them eventually became involved in the discussion. All that is, except for Victor Storm.

Finally, the time for the class was up. As everyone rose to leave, Victor caught the instructor sneaking a glance at him. The look on his face said he was wondering what Victor was doing here.

At the beginning of the class, Victor had wondered about that himself. Now he thought he knew: despite the inexperience of the other students and even the instructor, he thought he just might learn something.

CHAPTER THREE

In the parking garage at his parents' condominium complex, Victor put the suitcases down and watched his father shifting the other luggage in the back of the SUV. Though it was the end of August, the humidity and heat were both still up, and the old man's striped yellow golf shirt was beginning to look damp. Once he had the baggage arranged to his satisfaction, he turned back to Victor, who immediately picked up the suitcases and slid them into the vehicle.

While his father jockeyed the luggage some more, Victor shuffled uncomfortably on his feet. "Are you sure you want to do this?" he asked finally. "Move across the country, leave all your family and everything here behind?"

His father answered without looking back. "We aren't moving yet, Victor. We're just going to have a look."

"Mom said you were going to put a down payment on a place."

"Well, your mother has been talking about Florida for a long time. She thinks that's what she wants." He turned back to Victor and pushed the straw hat back on his head. Though his father's hairline was thinning and gray, it made Victor a little proud to see that he still kept his hair in a military haircut—a nice high and tight.

"It's hot and humid in Florida, too, you know."

His father gave him a gentle smile. "I know, Victor, and your mother will see that, too, when we get there. Nothing is set in stone yet. Personally, I believe that once we're there for a couple weeks, she'll see that the good parts aren't good enough to make up for the bad parts."

"The bad parts?"

"Yeah. She'll miss you, and your sister, your sister's kid, and your kids," he said, then added, "when they come around."

"Yeah," Victor said, looking away.

His father pressed the issue. "How is all that going? Have you gotten to see them lately?"

Victor shook his head. "She's still intent on staying in North Carolina, and she won't let them come back to visit. And she's telling her lawyer that she needs full custody." He scoffed. "She says I'm *dangerous*."

"Of course you are," his father said, a note of pride in his voice. "You were trained and paid well to be dangerous."

"That's not what she meant," Victor said, though his father already knew this.

His father nodded and gave him a serious look. "Still having the dreams?"

Victor couldn't make eye contact. "Sometimes."

"Maybe you should get a job growing things, put your energy into helping things live."

"You think that would help?"

His father smiled a bit sympathetically, blue eyes twinkling. "It worked for me."

They stood in awkward silence for a moment, then Victor's father turned back to the SUV and closed the hatch.

Right then, Victor's mother came around the corner from

the elevator, lugging two more suitcases. "Wait, Hank, we need to find room for these."

Victor's father looked at her narrowly. "It's only going to be two weeks, you know."

"I know, but if we find a place we like, we can just leave these there, and we won't have to move them later."

Victor's father sighed and reopened the hatch.

Victor's mother turned and looked critically at Victor. She'd taken to wearing sundresses and round hats ever since she'd begun talking about Florida, but she still carried herself with the proper dignity and poise of a military wife. "You look thin, Victor."

"I'm fine, Mom."

She sighed and tipped her head at him. "You could stay here while we're gone, you know. Maybe it would help to get a change of scenery, get out of that small apartment for a while."

"I like my small apartment."

"You said you liked the view from our balcony."

"I *do* like the view from your balcony, but I like to be in my own place."

"I know. It's just that your apartment is so tiny and ... low."

"Kathy, he's a grown man, retired now, even." Victor's father said, rejoining the conversation. "He wants to have his own life is all."

"Okay, okay," Victor's mother said. She stepped forward and put an arm around Victor's shoulder. "It was just an offer."

Victor's father turned back to the SUV, lowered the hatch carefully, and began to press it closed against the bulk of the luggage.

"So, you're going to look after our plants while we're gone?" Victor's mother asked him.

"Sure, sure. I'll come by every couple-three days to check on them, make sure they get what they need."

"What about Oscar?" his mother asked. "He really likes you, you know. Are you going to take him? Have you decided?"

Victor shook his head and smiled at her. "Samantha wants him."

Victor had exactly one sister, Samantha, and she lived exactly one bus ride away from him, in a townhouse in the Midtown neighborhood in St. Louis. She must have seen Victor walking up the sidewalk from the bus stop, because the door swung open in front of him as he passed the fountain in the front yard. "When are you going to get a car?"=

Victor smiled. "I'll get one as soon as I need one," he said, "but I don't see that day coming any time soon."

Samantha Storm stood in the doorway. Four years younger than Victor, she had a trim figure and straight blond hair. The finest of lines had begun to touch her face in the places where a smile creased her skin. When she was around Victor, she smiled a lot. She was frowning now, though. "Why did you tell them I'd take that dog? I don't want the dog. I thought you were going to take him."

Victor gave her a quick hug, and they stepped inside. "I thought Duncan liked him."

"Duncan *does* like him," she said. "The problem is, he's really latched onto Duncan, and now he won't let anyone else near him."

At that moment, Duncan came tearing out of his bedroom with Oscar, a scruffy West Highland White Terrier, right on his heels. "Uncle Bictor!" he shouted, wicked glee in his three-year-old eyes. Duncan ran across the living room and grabbed Victor around the legs in a big hug. Victor leaned down and patted him on the back. Oscar stopped short behind Duncan and growled at Victor.

"See what I mean?" Samantha said. Her words were in exasperation, but she was smiling.

Duncan let go of Victor and tore back across the living room to his bedroom, Oscar bounding beside him. Victor and Samantha smiled after them, then took seats on the couch and chair in the living room. Their conversation rapidly focused on their parents.

"Do you think they'll ever come back?" Samantha asked.

"They have to come back. Most of their stuff is still here."

"You know what I mean. Do you think they'll buy a place and move there, just come back here long enough to pack up a truck and be gone?"

Victor shrugged. "I don't know. I don't think so. I hope not."

"Yeah," Samantha said. This was well-covered ground, and neither of them had any new information. Time alone would tell. After only a moment, Samantha changed the subject. "Are you going to stay in their condo while they're gone?"

"No."

"Why not? It's big and nice, and you really like the view."

"I like being in my own place."

Samantha tried to look into Victor's eyes, but he wouldn't meet her gaze. "Are you still having those dreams?"

"Yeah. No," he lied. He'd mentioned to her before that he had bad dreams sometimes, and that they were of some of his action in Iraq, but he'd never been more specific, and he wasn't starting here and now.

"Did your philosophy class start yet?"

"Yeah."

"How's that going?"

"We've only had the one class so far, but I guess it's all right."

She tried to look into his eyes again. "Do you think it will help you?"

He hadn't told her his reasons for taking the class, and he was surprised and a little proud that she'd been able to figure it out on her own. "I don't know," he said. "Maybe. Probably not."

Samantha looked softly at Victor's face. "Maybe if you could find someone who was over there and talk to him about everything. Maybe that would help." She put her hand on his forearm. "Do you know anyone around here like that?"

Victor stared hard at the floor and actually considered it. It was what, three years since he'd gotten out? Yeah. Suddenly, he remembered something, and he felt his face brighten. "Maybe."

CHAPTER FOUR

Victor had served twenty years in the U.S. Army, and in those twenty years, he had met and worked with all kinds of people. Lots of strange coincidences turned up in that mix—he'd run into a former classmate at a base in Germany, for instance—but one guy that kept turning up in Victor's career was Lou Rollins.

Like Victor, Lou had grown up in St. Louis, but they had never seen each other before being assigned to the same paratrooper unit at Fort Bragg in North Carolina. After a few years of service together, both had reenlisted, but each from that point had gone in a different direction. Victor went on to become an instructor at the U.S. Army Airborne School, then to serve in the Special Forces. Lou, on the other hand, had joined a Military Police unit, then later become an investigator in the Criminal Investigation Division. Despite their separate paths, they had stayed in contact throughout their careers, and they had met each other for drinks and general rabble-rousing in Germany, Iraq, Turkey, England, Finland, and probably more places that Victor had forgotten.

Victor had last talked to Lou a few years earlier, shortly

before retiring. At that time, Lou had said that he, too, planned to retire in a couple of years and return to St. Louis.

Back in his apartment, Victor found Lou's mother's number—she still lived in the house where Lou had grown up—in the phone book. An hour later, Victor walked into Lou's office at police headquarters downtown.

"Victor Storm," Lou said when Victor walked in, showing him a big smile. "You made it out alive."

"I did, indeed," Victor said, smiling. Lou was a black man, and he had always had a deep voice, but it seemed to Victor that Lou's voice got deeper and richer every year. Now Victor struggled with the urge to call him 'Darth.' In the old days, he wouldn't have hesitated to sling a jibe like that Lou's way. Those days, however, were a long way in the past. "I see it didn't take you too long to get yourself set up here," Victor said. He glanced around the cluttered little office for effect. "I'm a little surprised you picked the Auto Theft Section, though."

"Yeah, well, I didn't pick it. I wanted Homicide or Vice—I've got almost ten years at CID, for Christ's sake—but they wanted me to work Auto for a while. They said they needed to wait for an opening, but I think they just want to see what I can do."

"So, you're showing them?"

"Yeah, I'm tearing it up."

They both laughed a moment, but the air between them had seemed to fill with an unspoken anxiety.

"So, what brings you down here?" Lou asked. "I don't suppose somebody stole your car."

"No," Victor said with a little grimace of a smile. "I—I just wanted to talk to an old friend."

That evening, Lou met Victor for dinner at a downtown restaurant with towering Palladian windows and a majestic view of the glittering city skyline. Victor had chosen this restaurant specifically for this view.

Victor's family had moved to St. Louis when he was a kid, when his father was assigned to the post he would ultimately hold until he retired. Immediately upon arriving, Victor had connected with this place on a deep level that he was at a loss to explain. Afterward, as an adult, no matter where he went in the world, no matter what wonders he saw, it was the St. Louis skyline, it was the myriad neighborhoods, it was the broad sweep of the Mississippi, it was the graceful, glittering, majestic arch that felt like home to him. Nowhere else on earth compared.

Victor got a table with a good view of the reassuring city, and he and Lou sat down to dinner. Victor hadn't told Lou he was having troubles, but Lou had seemed to sense it. Between mouthfuls of food and beer, they made small talk, catching up on events since they had seen each other last. Victor told Lou about taking the philosophy class, which got some laughs, and Lou told Victor about his father dying, which didn't.

"So, what are you doing with yourself these days, Victor?"

Victor shrugged. "I'm a student of the world."

"You're not working anywhere?"

Victor shook his head with a little smile. "I'm retired."

"Shit, I'm retired, too, Vic. We're all retired. That don't mean we don't have to work for a living. Unless you get a different kind of retirement pay than what I get."

"No, I just don't have expenses, that's all."

"No expenses?"

"No, I practice what they call 'voluntary simplicity.'"

Lou's frown deepened and turned serious. "What's that? Some kind of religious thing? You joined a cult?"

Victor smiled. "No, none of that. It just means I don't buy things I don't need, and I think very hard about what it is that I do need."

"What kind of things don't you need?"

"Well, I don't need a car, or cable television—"

"No car? No TV?"

"Well, I do *have* a television, just not cable. I don't really watch it that much, though."

"No car? How do you get around?"

"The bus runs everywhere I want to go, and if it doesn't, I rent a car."

"The bus? That's terrible."

"No, I like the bus."

Lou shook his head. "Shit, I couldn't do it."

Victor shrugged again. "I like it. Living simply lets me do what I want to do."

"Which is nothing."

Victor smiled again. Some people would never get it. "Which is to be a student of life."

"And philosophy."

"Yes, that, too."

Lou grunted into his beer. "Sounds like a cult."

Toward the end of the meal, they had run out of small talk—he was never very good at it anyway—and Victor had decided it was safe to ask Lou his question. He wiped his mouth with his napkin, looked around the room as if checking that the coast was clear, then leaned forward over the table and spoke in a low voice, "Do you ever have ... dreams about the things you did in the Army?"

Lou frowned across the table to see if Victor was serious. "Dreams? Not really." He looked down at his plate, then up again at Victor's face. "I take it you do?"

"Yeah," Victor said, then added, "mostly it's the same one,

over and over. Sometimes it's a little different, but it always goes the same way."

"Huh," Lou said. "And I take it this isn't a good dream, no cheerleaders, nothing like that?"

Victor shook his head.

Lou wiped his mouth with his napkin, threw it down on the table, and drained the last of the beer from his glass. "No, I don't have anything like that, but I wasn't really in the shit the way you were."

Victor said nothing, took a sip of his beer, and looked out the window at the horizon.

"Look, man, I'm sure it's nothing. A lot of ugly shit went down over there, and everywhere. I've heard of plenty of guys who get trouble sleeping when they get back. It's just what happens."

Victor glanced at Lou for a moment, then looked away again. "Most of the stuff—I don't have any problem letting it go. This one incident, though. I don't know if it's because it was Christmas Eve, or what, but it's stuck with me."

"Have you talked to the VA people about this?"

Victor frowned. "No."

"Go down and talk to them," Lou insisted. "That philosophy class is cute and all, but those kids ain't going to help you. They've never killed anybody on purpose before, and they never saw a buddy get killed, either. The guys at the VA, they know what to do. They deal with problems like this every day."

"I didn't say I was having problems. I said I was having dreams."

"Hmmph. Dreams like that sounds like a problem to me."

Victor's eyes stayed out the window, and his frown stayed in place.

"I'm serious, Vic. Go down there and talk to them."

"Ah, I don't know," Victor said. He sighed deeply and drank

down the last of his beer. "It's just some bad dreams, anyway. Nothing serious." He looked around the restaurant and bar as if seeing it for the first time. "Lou, let's get drunk and tear shit up, like the old days. Want to?"

Lou laughed his baritone hollow tunnel of a laugh. "I can't be doing that shit now. I'm a cop, Vic." He looked around at the quiet and dull patrons in the bar and restaurant, and his smile turned a bit mischievous. "Well, maybe just this once."

CHAPTER FIVE

A few months after he had moved into his apartment, Victor had discovered that the access door that led to the stairs to the roof had a bolt that didn't quite fit the frame correctly. If you inserted an ordinary credit card (of which Victor had exactly one), you could push the bolt back, and thereby gain access to the roof. After making this discovery, Victor found himself on the roof fairly frequently, sitting on the perimeter wall, looking out at the city and the river and the Arch and the horizon and all the stars above, just thinking about things.

The night after he'd met Lou for dinner downtown, Victor found himself on the roof again, sitting on the perimeter wall, watching the city lights, and thinking.

Seeing his old friend had felt good for his soul, but he still felt unsettled. Could he go to the VA hospital and tell them he was having bad dreams? He didn't think so. What would they do, anyway? No doubt their answer would be just some kind of therapy group, and some kind of "crazy" label for his file. He didn't think either one of those would help.

His father had suggested that he get a job growing things and had said that it had helped him. Victor's father had been in the Special Forces in the Vietnam War. He, too, had been in what Lou had referred to as "the shit." Had his father, too, been haunted by bad dreams?

Maybe. After retiring from the Army, Victor's father had pursued a career as a florist. Could Victor do that? No, he couldn't. He had set up his life with a minimum of expenses precisely so that he would not have to work, so that his time would be his own to use as he wished without answering to anyone. He wasn't going to give that up now, to go to work for someone else, just because of a few bad dreams.

Still, the idea of growing something, of doing something to make the world better, of redemption—he thought that might let him sleep better at night.

But what would he do? What *could* he do? The Army had taught him many skills, but it was these skills that had gotten him here.

———

A few days later, Victor was preparing to leave for his philosophy class when his father called with bad news.

"We looked at a bunch of places over here, and your mother fell in love with one of them."

Victor felt a bit like someone had kicked a chair out from under him. "She doesn't mind the heat and humidity?"

"It's actually been cool and nice while we've been here," his father said, sounding disappointed. "I keep telling her it isn't always like this, and even the weathermen are calling it unusual, but she won't hear it."

"Well, you haven't signed anything yet, have you?"

"No. She wanted to, but I told her we better keep looking around and not rush into anything."

"Wow," Victor said. This *was* bad news. "The drive out

there didn't make her realize how far she'd be from her—her family?"

"Nope. She says she's been cooped up in St. Louis for too long, and she wants to have some adventure before it's too late."

Victor said nothing. Adventure before it was too late was a concept he happened to agree with, but he didn't like his mother applying it to herself.

"We're going to go look at some more places tomorrow, then we're going to head up to St. Augustine this weekend. It's the oldest city on the continent, you know, supposed to be the most haunted city, too." He chuckled. "Should be fun."

"Then you'll be back next week, right?"

"Yeah, that's the plan."

Victor sighed. "I hope it's not just to pack up and leave."

"I hope so, too," said his father. "I hope so, too."

CHAPTER SIX

Colton Fischer had been lecturing about epistemology, the philosophical concept that seeks to answer the question of how you know something. This was all going well until someone in the back launched the question: Does God exist? Immediately, the order in the class fell apart.

A well-dressed and impeccably groomed young man who always sat center front of the class, and who Victor had come to know was named Dan and to refer to as "Dapper Dan," piped up: "We know that God exists because the Bible tells us he does."

Several people groaned.

"How do you know that's right?" someone said.

"Because it says it is," Dapper Dan said.

More people groaned.

"If God exists," said a very round young black girl who Victor had come to know was named Loretta, "why is there so much misery in the world?"

"An excellent question," Colton Fischer said, then added with a slight frown, "not really epistemological, though."

A round-eyed white girl named Kerri who always sat next

to Dan spoke over her shoulder at the rest of the class without turning to meet their eyes. "You can see that God exists because you can see him in the face of every newborn baby."

People groaned.

"Uh," Colton Fischer said.

"Your butt exists," someone muttered.

A flurry of laughter swept through the class at this.

"This is a dumb question," Dapper Dan said in the direction of Colton Fischer. "We know that God exists because he tells us he does in the Bible. How could he tell us that if he didn't exist? Why would he lie?"

To Victor's dismay, the discussion never really got any better than that.

After class, Victor met Lou again for a couple of beers, this time at a little jazz bar.

To the right inside the front door, a glossy wooden bar ran the length of the room. Just in from that, separated from the bar stools by a walkway, a row of booths sat in a line. A scattering of tables filled the rest of the room to the left. There were no pool tables in the place, just a pinball machine and an electronic dart board in a little corner down at the end of the booths. In the near left corner of the room, the round tables gave way to a little wooden stage. Some nights this bar had live jazz bands playing here. Tonight the crowd was light, and the stage was empty.

Both Victor and Lou, being military veterans, wanted to sit at one of the end booths so they could see the whole room, but neither wanted to be the one to sit with his back to the little crowd. They finally compromised, sitting at the middle booth and watching each other's back, just like the old days.

Right away a waitress with a maroon smock took their order and brought them two tall glasses of beer.

Victor made small talk by telling Lou about Dapper Dan.

Lou shook his head. "Sounds like a damn Mormon."

Victor smiled. "I think you may be right."

Victor hadn't laughed in class, but now they both laughed about the snide remarks people had been sending up.

"So, is that class helping you any?" Lou asked.

Victor shrugged. "The conversation isn't, but the concepts and approaches might be."

Lou grunted a bit disdainfully. "Did you go down to the VA office like I told you?"

Victor frowned and shook his head.

"Man, you need to get your ass out of that philosophy class and down to the VA center."

Victor raised his eyebrows and took a drink of his beer. "My father said I should get a job growing things like he did. Said it worked for him."

"Is that what you're going to do, then? Get a job at the Botanical Garden, or work at your father's flower shop?"

Victor shrugged and looked away. "I don't know."

———

The next day, Victor lay around his apartment all day, the television flickering on his face, not really watching it. He thought the whole day that what he should be doing was calling the VA center and making an appointment, but he didn't do it.

The day after that, he read his philosophy text for a while, and he became absorbed in it, particularly by the elusive nature of the definition of *knowledge*. Motivated by this, and wanting to know more of the varied ideas on the subject, he went down to the central branch of the public library and looked for books about it. This was a frustrating activity because it seemed that every question was answered with two more questions. After a while, Victor began to feel overwhelmed.

Before he realized it, night had fallen. His examination of the books had shown him that, of all the books on philosophy, the one that best explained the main concepts most clearly was the textbook he already owned.

Strangely, this knowledge gave him a small measure of satisfaction.

He walked home, textbook under his arm, feeling hopeful, almost happy even, for the first time in several days, maybe weeks, maybe months.

All that vanished when he found his apartment open and his sister waiting for him inside. Her eyes were red and puffy, mascara down both cheeks like he'd never seen it before.

"It's Mom and Dad," she said, her voice breaking. "They're gone."

CHAPTER SEVEN

In the dream, his own panic and that of his team feel thick in the air, almost palpable. The man speaks in a steady stream of Arabic, the words too fast and foreign to understand.

They shout at him to stop, to put his hands up.

The man keeps moving to their right.

He sees the man now over the sights of his rifle. Unable to tear his eyes from the man, he doesn't see at first what the man is moving toward: a telephone on a table.

They shout at him to stop, to put his hands up. The man never stops chattering Arabic at them, a deluge of consonants.

He keeps moving toward the phone.

Suddenly there's movement in the doorway to the left. A woman appears, spewing long torrents of Arabic at them. Her arms move. He sees she is holding a rifle. He sees the end of it coming up, the black hole in the end of the barrel rising to add its voice to the Arabic chorus.

He feels his heart stop.

Around him, he hears voices shouting *Stop!* in Arabic.

In his head, he is shouting, pleading with her to stop. Even in his head, the words are in Arabic.

The rifle keeps coming up.

He wakes up, the dream falling away in echoes, replaced by the dark and tiny apartment.

The word *Stop!* is on his lips in Arabic. He whispers it to the darkness.

———

Victor would later recall that getting through the next several days was the roughest experience of his life, harder than any Special Forces training exercise, more difficult even than combat had been.

The hardest part, probably, was the first: flying out to Jacksonville to provide positive identification of the bodies. His mother's face had been swollen, distorted. It looked like she had been crying. His father's face was harder to recognize. He had to look at it more closely than he wanted to, hoping beyond hope that the corpse with the lip cut wide open and the black round hole in the forehead over the left eye wasn't really his father.

Victor would never know how he made it through that.

Next, he had to fly back to St. Louis, with the bodies, for the funeral. Years earlier, his parents had bought plots in a cemetery near the red brick townhouse where Victor and Samantha had grown up. Seeing the little crowd of people at the cemetery, Victor could clearly remember the day his parents had told him about buying the plot, could remember them taking him and Samantha to show it to them. Victor had been in high school at the time, and the time of actually using the plot was decades away, a longer period of time than he could imagine ever passing. Now, he couldn't believe how quickly it had all gone.

Samantha wore a black dress, black gloves, and a black lace

veil. Victor was struck by how beautiful she looked, then felt guilty for thinking so.

Samantha had dressed Duncan in a little black suit. Being three years old, he couldn't possibly understand what was going on, but he seemed to know that the occasion was somber, and he stood straight and brave.

Victor's wife Angelina had—reluctantly—brought their daughters to the funeral as well. The three of them were a resplendent vision of mourning in black dresses, but Angelina kept them mostly away from Victor, seemingly—and correctly—worried about what he might do. Afterward, Victor thought he should have had something wise or comforting to say to his daughters, but at the time his brain was a tangled mess of tasks and emotions swirling together, and he felt as though he was barely keeping his head above water.

Several men from his father's old unit showed up for the proceedings. Victor was sure he had been introduced to some of them before, and he should have known them, but he recognized none.

Lou Rollins came to the funeral as well, wearing a dark suit and sunglasses. Victor was glad to see him there.

Because Victor's father had retired from the Army, a detail had been sent to perform a three-gun salute and play taps. Victor had witnessed the ceremony several times before, of course, but he had never been terribly affected by it. Price of war and that kind of thing. Hearing taps played for his father—for both his parents at once—he got lightheaded and started to wobble. Lou grabbed Victor's arm to steady him, and Victor got through it.

The Army detail took the flag from the coffin, folded it, and tried to present it to him. He couldn't take it. He shook his head and directed it off to his sister.

Later, he would feel guilty about that, too.

After the services, as the little crowd was getting into their vehicles to leave, Victor looked to join his wife and daughters, but they had already walked back to the path and were getting into her car. As the car began to drive away, Victor saw the faces of his daughters turn to him in the passenger windows. He waved to them, and his heart melted just a bit as he saw their hands come up in the windows and return his wave.

"What's the status, man?" Lou asked, suddenly at his side. "Did they get the bastard yet?"

Victor turned to him and shook his head.

"What's the problem?"

"I don't know," Victor said. "But I'm going to find out." His jaw set in determination. "I'm flying to Jacksonville tonight."

CHAPTER EIGHT

Back at his apartment, Victor lit a cigarette and paced the floor. In the Special Forces, he'd been trained to be independent, aloof. Survival, escape, resistance, evasion, with the team if you had it, but ultimately on your own. In the time since he'd retired, he'd tried to reverse that training, to become more sociable, less detached. For a while, he'd thought that he was making progress.

The murder of his parents had changed all that. His senses felt sharper, keener. After quitting years ago, he was smoking again. He felt younger, more raw. He had this nagging fear that he might be moving in the wrong direction. But it sure felt good to be moving.

He noticed the light on his answering machine blinking and pushed the button.

Hello, this message is for Victor Storm. My name is Rebecca Dubois. I'm a reporter for the St. Louis Examiner, and I'd like to do a feature about your parents—

Victor killed the message with the delete button.

Victor felt cold, efficient, and lethal on the trip to Jacksonville. Lean and rigid. Bus to airport. Plane to Jacksonville. Rental car. Hotel.

The only part of the trip that really didn't fit him was the plane ride. He had weapons at home, but of course he couldn't take them on the plane, didn't even dare to try. In the hotel he got a room on the top floor, overlooking the ocean. That first night, he stood on the balcony, watching the moonlight-crested waves twinkling up to shore. He could *make* weapons, of course. The Army had taught him to make weapons of nearly anything, and even in this hotel room, there were any number of things that could be used to kill: a cut length of phone cord could strangle, a broken splinter of dresser drawer could stab, an unscrewed table leg could bludgeon, a phone book dropped into a pillowcase could stun, even pulverize.

In the morning he quickly located police headquarters and parked the rental car. Walking from the parking lot to the short row of steps up the front of the white stone and gleaming glass building, he quickly found his shirt damp. The heat and humidity had returned. He resisted the urge to rage at the universe, to ask why the suffocating combination had been put on pause long enough for his mother to consider moving here, long enough for her to die. These thoughts he would not let into his head.

He marched up the steps, pushed the heavy, black glass door open, crossed the clean tile lobby to the front desk, and asked to see the detective in charge of the investigation. The uniformed officer at the desk looked at him. Victor could see questions in the man's head, questions he was supposed to ask. Something in Victor's demeanor, though, must have convinced him not to ask. Instead, he simply picked up the phone, punched some numbers, spoke in a low voice for a moment, and asked Victor to wait.

The investigating detective turned out to be a polished young man named Ortega. Dressed in a casual shirt and slacks, with a badge on one side of his belt and a handgun in a holster on the other, he strode confidently into the lobby and shook Victor's hand firmly.

"As I told you on the phone, Mr. Storm, there is no reason to come down here. We'll get the person who did this."

"Have you got him yet?"

"No."

"Then that's why I'm here."

Ortega stiffened. "Are you saying that you intend to catch the perpetrator?"

Victor thought of a phone cord, a splinter of dresser drawer, a table leg. "Yes."

Ortega's brown eyes connected with Victor's. He seemed to be trying to gauge the seriousness, the sanity he saw there. Then his expression softened, and he put a hand on Victor's shoulder. "Why don't we talk in my office?"

Victor looked around quickly, as if coming out of a daze. He looked at Ortega again, trying to emote calm control. "All right."

Ortega led the way down a side hall past some quiet offices to a little room that was as neat and orderly as Ortega himself. Closing the door behind them, he gestured for Victor to sit in the chair in front of the desk, then moved around the desk to sit. Through the big window behind the detective, Victor could almost see back to his hotel and the ocean.

The detective leaned forward with his elbows on the desk, hands folded together casually. "This case has generated a lot of interest. I even got a call from an FBI man up in D.C. offering to help us out." He waved a hand in the direction of Washington, a brushing-off motion. "I told him the same thing I'm going to tell you, Mr. Storm, which is that the investigation is going very well. The witnesses at the scene provided us with some very solid leads, and we expect to make an arrest at any moment."

Victor sat back in his chair. Was he ... disappointed? That's what it felt like. He looked back at Ortega. "What happened to them?"

Ortega looked blankly at Victor for a moment, trying to read his expressions, clearly figuring out what to say. "Mr. Storm, your parents were killed in a restaurant robbery—"

"I know the sanitized version," Victor snapped. "I want to know what happened."

Ortega took the interruption in stride. He paused a moment before beginning again. "Your parents went to a restaurant, apparently to have dinner. While they were waiting for their food to arrive, a man wearing a black ski mask entered the building carrying a gun. After taking the cash from the register, he began going from table to table, demanding the wallets and purses of the patrons. When he got to your parents' table, there was a scuffle, and your parents were shot. After the shooting, the perpetrator fled the restaurant on foot."

Victor felt lightheaded. "Why did he shoot them?"

Ortega's eyes tried to connect with Victor's again. "Mr. Storm, I think it might be better if we don't—"

"No," Victor said. "I want to know."

The detective closed his mouth, regarding him.

"I want to know."

Ortega stood up and looked out the tall window, considering. After a moment he turned back to Victor with a polite but grim smile. "All right."

CHAPTER NINE

Detective Ortega told the details straightforward and plainly.

The other patrons of the restaurant had surrendered their wallets without incident, but Victor's father had refused. According to the witnesses, he simply told the robber to go to hell. The robber stepped forward, apparently to try to forcibly take the old man's wallet. The witnesses said it looked like Victor's father wasn't scared by this, like he had been taunting the robber, trying to get him to move closer.

"He was," Victor said at this point. "He was an old Special Forces soldier. He knew what he was doing. He needed him to get closer, to get him off his plan, so he could disarm him."

Ortega said nothing to respond to this, looking at Victor almost sympathetically before continuing the story.

When the robber reached the table, there was a scuffle. Victor's father made a grab for the gun, but the robber jumped back. The witnesses said that at this point the old man jumped up from his seat and started to lunge at the robber, but he had been partially blocked by Victor's mother, who had also leaped to her feet and was yelling for him to stop.

"That's my mother," Victor said, shaking his head. "She

always wants to protect him—" He cut himself off, realizing that he was speaking of her in the present tense, and not wanting to accept that it was no longer appropriate. He looked down at the floor and swallowed hard. "She should have let him go. He knew what he was doing."

Detective Ortega fell silent at his desk.

Victor swam in his thoughts for a moment before he realized the narrative had stopped. He looked up at Ortega. "And?"

Ortega looked at Victor.

"Go on," Victor insisted.

Ortega silently sighed and finished the story.

Witnesses said that that's when the robber shot. The first shot hit his father in the head, and he fell to the floor. His mother threw herself on the body, screaming, and the robber shot her once in the back before running off. By the time the paramedics arrived, Victor's father was dead. Victor's mother died on the way to the hospital.

Victor stared hard at the floor. "Why did he shoot her?"

Ortega shook his head gently. "No one knows."

Victor stood up quickly and paced to the door of the office and back to the chair. He reached up and squeezed the back of his neck for a moment, then stood rigidly facing Ortega. "What are these leads you have, the ones you said were solid?"

Now the detective sat back in his chair, hands in his lap. "Mr. Storm, I can't discuss the details of an ongoing investigation."

"Don't give me that," Victor snapped. "My parents were killed, and I want to know what you're doing to catch the guy that did it."

Ortega sighed deeply again. He leaned forward and put his elbows back on the desk.

"A couple of miles from the restaurant, on the night of the

murder, a man stopped at a convenience store to get some gas and some cigarettes. The clerk thought it was suspicious when the man came in to pay and had two wallets, so he noted the make and model of the car, and got part of the license plate. When he saw the news of the robbery on television, he gave us a call."

Victor nodded. "And?"

"And, using what he told us about the car, we were able to identify an owner, and therefore, a suspect. He had moved since registering the car, but we were able to get his address through ... other means."

Victor paced to the door and back, frowning hard.

"The suspect was not at his address, but we have a unit watching the apartment."

"You don't think he skipped out?"

"No, we don't think so. We expect to be making an arrest, literally, any minute."

Victor paced to the door and back again, stopping squarely in front of Ortega's desk. "What is his name?"

Ortega tipped his head away to the side. "I think we'd better—"

Victor put a hand on Ortega's desk and shook his head. "What's the name?"

Ortega sat back in his chair. This was the question he had the hardest time with. Finally, perhaps because he knew that the units were watching his house and he felt an arrest was imminent, he said, "Dario Mullen."

CHAPTER TEN

Victor left the name of his hotel with Ortega before leaving the police station. His head swam with the details he'd learned. He intended to drive straight back to his hotel, but instead, he found himself driving through the streets of Jacksonville. He wondered where he was going, but he didn't try to stop.

He thought of his father, the old Special Forces man. He would have gotten that gun. Victor was sure of it. He had turned sixty-five a few months earlier, but Victor would still have picked him to win any fight he got into. Once you went through Special Forces training, and you applied that training in real life, it stayed with you.

It was his mother who had gotten in the way. In his mind, he could imagine her arm on his wrist. He could imagine his father reeling suddenly, trying to put himself between his wife and the robber. How could Victor blame her, though? She'd been trying to protect the man she loved. When the shit hits the fan, people react without thinking, doing what they've been trained to do. Victor's father reacted as a Special Forces soldier. His mother reacted as, well, his mother. No one was to blame. It was simply a terrible combination. Things worked out that way sometimes.

Victor found himself turning off the main streets of Jacksonville. He noticed he was slowing down in front of apartment complexes.

He seemed to be looking for the killer.

This would not do. To begin with, he had no idea what the killer looked like. He surely wouldn't be wearing the black ski mask, and there was little chance he'd be wearing a sports jersey with the name *Mullen* on the back. For another thing, there had to be hundreds of apartment complexes in Jacksonville. If he thought it would help, he would surely drive past every single one of them. He did not, however, seriously think it would help.

He needed to stop driving and come up with a plan. He needed space to think and the resources to plot. One place fit that description: the hotel.

Though it had seemed that he must have been driving for hours, when he turned back toward his hotel, he found that he was only a few blocks from it. By the time he got back to his room, it was still barely eleven in the morning.

Back up in his room, he opened the sliding glass door and stood out on the balcony. What was it, exactly, that he hoped to do? He knew that he wanted to find out where Mullen lived and to go there, but what for? Ortega had told him there were units watching the place. Even if he wanted to go there and confront him, the police would surely nab Mullen as soon as he returned. Was he going to go there, then, and simply watch them make the arrest?

Yes, he thought that's exactly what he wanted to do. He told himself that Mullen had already killed two people, and he just might get lucky and kill or otherwise get away from the police who were waiting to arrest him. If that happened,

Victor could be there, waiting to apprehend him—and applying whatever level of force was necessary to do so.

So, that was his plan: go to Mullen's place, watch the police watching for Mullen, and hope for the worst. It wasn't the best plan, but it was better than sitting here.

The only problem was that he still had no idea where Mullen lived. For a plan that involved going there, that was a big problem. He didn't think Ortega was going to give him that information, even if Victor called and carefully explained his plan. So, how was he going to find that out?

Victor lit a cigarette and stared out at the white lines of waves rolling in over the blue ocean, considering this. The answer seemed to be within his reach, but where?

Ortega had said they had found Mullen's address through "other means." What did that mean? If the government databases didn't have a real address, what did? Surely not—

Victor threw his cigarette over the balcony and went back into the room. On the shelf above the coat rack by the front door, he found the phone book.

There it was: Mullen, Dario. And it had an address.

Victor tore the page out of the phone book, folded it, and put it in his back pocket. A little smile lifted the corner of his mouth.

He was about to head out the door when the phone rang.

He stopped in his tracks and stared at the phone. Only two people knew where he was staying: Samantha, and Ortega.

It was Ortega. "I told you we'd get him."

CHAPTER ELEVEN

Back down at police headquarters, Victor was greeted by Detective Ortega, who was absolutely beaming. "I told you we'd get him," he said. "I told you."

Victor was not beaming. "I want to see him."

A frown drew over Ortega's face. "We can't do that."

"He killed my parents."

"Which is precisely why we can't let you near him."

Victor turned away. It had been foolish to ask, foolish to get his hopes up. Now was not the time to be foolish. He turned back to Ortega. "You're sure it's the right guy?"

Ortega nodded, smiling again. "He broke down and confessed everything in the car on the way down here. Told the officers everything, crying like a baby." Ortega was happy about this. "Plus, they found quite a bit of cash at his apartment."

"Wallets?"

"No, no wallets, but they did find a black ski mask."

Victor nodded. "What about the gun?"

"Dario told them he threw the gun in a ditch not too far

from the scene of the crime. We've got people out there looking for it right now."

"Just 'a ditch'? Nothing more specific?"

Ortega smiled warmly. "Don't worry, Mr. Storm. We'll find it."

Victor turned away and stared out the window for a minute. "So, what's next?"

Ortega sighed heavily again, but this time it was a sigh of relief. "Now we turn everything over to the District Attorney. He'll take it from here. It could go to trial, but in this case, with him already confessing on the way down here and all, I don't think so."

Victor stared out the window another minute, seeing nothing. He turned back to Ortega. "So, what now? More waiting?"

Ortega smiled gently. "It will take a little time, Mr. Storm, but the wheels are in mo—"

The phone on Ortega's desk rang. Both men looked at the blinking red lights. Ortega appeared for a second to consider not answering it, then held a finger up to Victor and picked it up.

Immediately a smile took over the bottom half of his face. "They did?" he said into the phone. "It was?" The smile grew wider. "Excellent." He hung up the phone and turned to Victor. "They found the gun."

———

"So, what happens next?" Samantha asked on the phone that evening. She sounded tired, and to Victor it seemed that her voice was distant, at the end of a long tunnel. He wanted to be with her, but he was still in his hotel in Jacksonville.

"Next is the arraignment," Victor said. "Tomorrow morning."

"And then what? The trial?"

"Well, they tell me it depends on how he pleads, but they seem to think, since he's already confessed, that he'll likely plead guilty."

"I hope so."

Victor said nothing. He had been thinking about this all day, and he wasn't sure what he was hoping for now.

"What are you going to do?"

"Well, I'm going to the arraignment tomorrow morning, that's for sure. They wouldn't let me see the bastard today, but the arraignment is public, and they can't stop me from going."

Samantha paused a moment. "Are you sure that's a good idea?"

"Yeah, I'm sure," Victor said. "I want to see him, and I want him to see me."

"You want him to know how much Mom and Dad meant to you?"

Victor's voice turned cold. "Not exactly."

Samantha seemed to consider asking Victor what he meant by that, then decided to let it go. "I don't think he's going to plead guilty."

"What? Why?"

"Because no one ever pleads guilty anymore. He'll plead innocent, then try to get off."

"But—he already confessed; they already found the gun."

"I know," Samantha said, sounding disgusted, "but I just have this feeling. I'm sure he'll plead innocent."

Victor felt this give him hope, though for what he did not know. At least, he did not allow himself to think about it. He said nothing.

"What are you going to do if he does plead innocent?" Samantha asked. "Stay there for the trial?"

"I—I haven't thought about it. I guess so."

"You should come back here. The trial probably won't be for a while, and you have your philosophy classes to go to."

"Um, yeah. I've been thinking about that, and I think I should just drop the class."

"Victor, no. You like the class. I got the feeling you were finding something there to help you with ... things."

"I don't see how I can continue going. Even if the trial isn't right away, I've already missed classes to deal with all this."

"Still, I *like* you taking that class."

Victor sighed silently into the phone. "We'll see."

———

Victor met the prosecutor from the District Attorney's office before the arraignment. He was an older white man named Gordon Sham. He had a bald head, he wore an immaculate white suit, he smelled like expensive cologne, and he had the bearing of someone who took no shit. Victor liked him right away. He didn't trust him, but he liked him.

While they waited for the defendant to appear, Victor looked around the room. The judge was a woman with red hair going gray in a bob haircut. Victor didn't see her smile at anyone, and he liked that. A couple of bailiffs worked behind the judge, and a mousy little court reporter sat off to the side with her little machine. Victor seemed to be the only one attending the proceedings who was not working.

Gordon Sham had told Victor that Dario Mullen was to be represented by a court-appointed attorney. Across the aisle at the defendant's table, Victor saw a little man with a cheap blue suit and a weasel face: the public defender—but not, Victor reminded himself, the enemy.

A few minutes before the arraignment was set to begin, the bailiffs swung open a side door and a wiry white guy with a three-day scruffy beard, four-day greasy hair, and two-week dirty clothes shuffled into the room. Dario Mullen.

Victor stared daggers at him as he made his way over the defense table with the public defender, who greeted him curtly.

Dario glanced over at the prosecutor's table but made eye contact with no one. He kept his eyes mostly on the floor.

Once everything started happening, it happened very fast. The judge read off the case number and the charges and asked Dario Mullen how he plead.

Not guilty.

The judge looked at some papers on her desk and set a date for the trial to begin in mid-December.

She rapped her gavel, and that was it. The bailiffs came to take Dario Mullen away, and the lawyers began putting their papers back into their briefcases.

"But," Victor complained to Gordon Sham in a low voice. "That's three months away!"

"We're pretty lucky," Sham said, glancing up from his papers with a frown. "It's usually longer." He shook his head a bit. "Doesn't look like we'll get this wrapped up before Christmas."

So, Samantha had been right.

"What am I supposed to do in the meantime?" Victor asked.

Sham looked at him seriously and put his hand on Victor's shoulder. "Everything is under control here," he said. "Go home."

———

In the dream, he's speaking tersely to the Iraqi man. "Stop! Put your hands up."

Behind him, he hears the youngest member of the team beginning to lose it. "Oh, no. We're blown!"

Someone else shouts quietly: "Don't let him get to that phone!"

He sees the phone now, on a table to the right. The man is still moving toward it, saying something in Arabic too quickly for them to understand.

A woman appears in the doorway, suddenly spewing a torrent of Arabic at them.

The man reaches the phone.

His team is behind him. He's the only one who can act.

Everything happens so fast.

He feels the rifle kick in his hands.

The Iraqi man's head jerks and a spray of crimson paints the wall behind him.

The woman brings the rifle up.

His rifle kicks again.

CHAPTER TWELVE

This time, Victor's philosophy class was discussing war.

"What about war?" Colton Fischer asked. "Can war ever be ethical?"

"It depends on the reasons," someone suggested.

"So, you're saying that war is ethical if it is justified?" Colton Fischer restated. "What kinds of things might justify a war, then?"

"Oil," someone said.

People laughed.

Dapper Dan, who seemed to Victor, in spite of his spirited views on religious concepts, to be headed toward a law degree, of course wanted his opinion known. "If the action is authorized by the proper channels, then it's justified."

Colton raised his eyebrows. "The proper channels? And what might those be?"

"CNN," someone said.

"MTV."

Groans and happy chuckles now. At least they knew what those were.

"What about Congress?" Loretta asked. "Or the President?"

Colton Fischer shrugged. "Does their approval make a war ethical?"

"Yes," Dapper Dan said. "As long as they're acting within the law, which, as we've already discussed, is built on the commandments in the Bible."

Victor was very happy he had missed that class.

"So, you're saying," Colton Fischer restated again, "that as long as the Congress or the President give their approval, then it's acceptable to go into another country and kill their people?"

"Yes," said Dapper Dan, who seemed proud to think he had reached this conclusion logically.

"Wait a minute," Victor said.

Every head in the class turned to look at him. He had never spoken in class before.

"Are you saying," Victor continued, "that occasionally it's all right to go kill people, and that you know when that is? Do you suppose any of those people agree with you?"

Dapper Dan stood his ground. "It doesn't matter if they agree. As long as we're acting in accordance with our laws, which are built on the Bible—"

"What are you going to tell their children?" Victor demanded.

Dapper Dan said nothing.

"Are you going to just explain to their children that it's okay that you killed their parents because your laws said it was okay, your *religion*? They will *never* accept that."

"Philosophy isn't about winning the argument," Dapper Dan retorted. "It's about being right."

"And what would you know about being right?" Victor shot back. "You think you know what's right, and that just because you can sit in class here and point at your Bible that makes you right?"

Colton Fischer raised a hand and opened his mouth to speak, but Victor cut him off before he even got started.

"I tell you what," Victor said, still talking to Dapper Dan. "You go there. You go there and kill some people. Then go and face their children. After that, you can come back here and tell me how right you feel. But until you've done some of that, just shut the fuck up."

———

Lou Rollins listened to the story, trying to drink his beer and smile at the same time. "What'd he have to say to that?" he asked when Victor had finished.

Victor shrugged. "I don't know. I was so pissed off by that time—and embarrassed, frankly—that I just walked out."

"And you ain't been back since?"

"That was just yesterday. There hasn't been a class since then."

They were back at the little bar, at the center table again. This time, what looked like a jazz trio was preparing to play. Lou took another drink of his beer. "Don't worry about it, Victor. In the first place, you're right. What have any of those little punks ever seen?"

"Yeah."

"Besides, you're probably stressed out about the trial coming up, and I can guarantee none of them ever had to deal with something like that, neither."

"Yeah, that," Victor said. "I got a call from the prosecutor over there today. The gun doesn't match."

"You said they found the gun in the ditch where he told them."

"Well, apparently he didn't know precisely what ditch it was, he just knew the general area. They searched there and found one. They thought it was it."

"But it wasn't?"

Victor shook his head, frowned, and took a sip of beer. "They said the ballistics test proved it couldn't be the same one."

"What? They have guns floating around in all the ditches over in Jacksonville?"

Victor shrugged. "Maybe."

Deep furrows creased Lou's brow. "Seems like they should have found that out right away. Ballistics tests don't take that long."

"I asked them about that, and they never gave me a straight answer." Victor sighed. "I guess they figured this case was a lock, so the ballistics test wasn't a priority."

"What happens now? They didn't let the guy go, did they?"

"No, they still have his confession, and they went back to look for the gun again."

"But it's been several weeks now. Who knows if it's even still there?" Lou sounded as agitated as Victor felt.

"Right."

"Plus, it looks like they'll find a gun in every ditch they check, and it will take a while to sort out which one is right."

Victor didn't smile. They drank their beer for a while in silence, watching the jazz trio setting up their instruments on the little wooden stage. The energetic young black man with a purple pork pie hat seemed to be the leader of the group. Victor surveyed the instruments they were assembling—drums, electric guitar, bass guitar, keyboards, harmonica, cowbell, even a trumpet—and thought the band leader was going to need all the energy he could muster.

"So, are you going to go back to that philosophy class," Lou asked, "make sure them kids know what's what?"

"I don't know, Lou," Victor said. "Maybe it's because I'm only forty-one and I'm already retired, or maybe it's because my wife left and took the kids, or maybe it's everything, but sometimes I just don't know which way is up anymore."

"I hear that," Lou said.

"I thought that by taking this philosophy class, maybe I could find a way to think about things, find out how other people have thought about things before."

Lou nodded and said nothing.

"But the way it's been going lately, I just don't know. It seems like the instructor there knows some things. But every time we hit on some logic, the whole class takes it and runs the other way."

Lou took a drink of his beer and frowned.

"I took the class because I wanted to find out the truth, to find out, despite the things I've been taught and learned on my own, what the real truth might be." Victor took a sip of his beer, searching for words. "It seems to me that everyone else is only looking for ways to justify what they think they already know." Another sip. "And any argument, no matter how illogical or contrived, is good enough for them."

"So," ventured Lou, "you're not going back?"

Onstage, the drummer rapped out a few test beats on his kit. The leader of the band now had the guitar slung around himself on one side, the trumpet on the other, the harmonica on a cord around his neck, and keyboards at the ready at his side. This was either going to be very good, or very bad.

Victor shook his head. "I don't know."

Colton Fischer wrote the word in big chalk letters on the blackboard: *JUSTICE*. He turned to the class and pointed back at the board. "Anyone have an idea how to define that word?"

Loretta looked stumped. Dapper Dan looked thoughtful. No one, for a change, had any smart-ass answers to shout out.

"It means," Victor said, "getting what you deserve. If you do something wrong, and you have to pay for it, that's justice."

Everyone turned to look at him, to see if this was perhaps the beginning of another outburst.

Colton Fischer nodded with a little smile. "Does anyone have anything to add to that?"

"Prison?" suggested Loretta.

Colton Fischer raised his eyebrows. "Is prison required?"

Thoughtful murmurs.

"How about," suggested Dapper Dan, "whatever punishment is decided on by our judicial system."

Colton Fischer turned to him. "Do you think that's true? Does justice require a *system*?"

"Yes," Dapper Dan said, nodding resolutely and adding in a grand aside to the class, "and our judicial system is the best in the world."

Colton Fischer tipped his head. "What about before our judicial system existed? Was there no justice then?"

Dapper Dan frowned.

From the back of the room, someone finally thought of something smart-ass to say: "There was hamburger justice."

"Even today," Colton Fischer continued, "what about other parts of the world, or even here? Does justice require a system? Could it be the work, for instance, of just one man?"

"No," Dapper Dan said flatly. "One man can't be judge, jury, and executioner."

A murmur of support swept through the class.

"Some people would say," Colton Fischer said thoughtfully, "that 'justice' is a philosophical concept, but 'the justice system' is a bureaucracy created for the enforcement of laws, which usually have very little in connection with philosophical justice."

"That's not true," Dapper Dan said.

"In fact," Colton Fischer continued, ignoring Dan, "many people have pointed out instances where the justice system has *prevented* justice from coming into the world, by preventing individuals from acting, yet botching cases themselves, either by accident or for some other gain."

The class was quiet, considering this.

"Some people wonder whether a bureaucracy can *ever* produce true justice, and sometimes that's an easy thing to wonder." Colton Fischer looked around at the room, smiling because he had them all speechless. "So these people wonder: if justice can't come from a bureaucracy, is it ever *truly* more than the work of one person, whether that person is a prosecutor, a detective, or even an outlaw vigilante?"

CHAPTER THIRTEEN

Victor's plane touched down in Jacksonville early in the evening. It had been rough waiting, but Samantha and Lou and even the damn philosophy classes had helped him to keep his sanity. Now it was time for the trial.

He checked into the same hotel where he'd stayed before. Only a few months had passed since he'd been here, but it seemed longer. The air here was warmer than the chill already present in St. Louis, but it was no longer as oppressive as it had been in early September.

Victor felt calmer than he had before. He didn't like to think that he was coming to grips with losing his parents—he liked to think that he'd never recover from that, that he'd always have it as a badge of honor, or a crutch. But he did feel less of a sense of urgency to the matter. The wheels were in motion, and everything was going as planned by the system.

He called Gordon Sham after he'd gotten settled in his hotel room and confirmed that the trial was still set to begin in the morning.

"Still on," Sham told him. "Eight o'clock sharp."

"Did they find the gun yet?" Victor asked.

"No, but don't worry about that," Sham said. "We've got a solid case without it. Very solid."

Victor called Samantha, too. She sounded relieved that it was almost over. "Be strong," she said.

CHAPTER FOURTEEN

When Victor arrived at court the next morning, however, he found precious little to be strong about, except patience.

It turned out that the trial proper wasn't getting underway, but that first he'd have to sit through jury selection.

"All part of the routine," Gordon Sham said, and clapped him on the shoulder. "All according to plan. Takes only a few hours."

By noon, however, this seemed overly optimistic. Gordon Sham had arrived to select the jury members, but the public defender, it seemed, was only there to reject them. Potential juror after potential juror stood up for questioning, to be approved by Gordon Sham but rejected by the public defender.

"Racial bias," he said.

"Biased because of military service."

"Biased by gun ownership."

When lunchtime rolled around, only one juror had been selected: a scruffy-looking, unemployed white guy who needed a shave and, likely, a shower.

"Does it always take this long?" Victor asked Gordon Sham

under his breath, as the public defender rejected yet another potential juror.

"Don't worry about it," Sham said. "All part of the process."

As the afternoon rolled on, however, even Gordon Sham seemed to lose his patience. "Your honor," he complained to the judge, "I'm starting to believe that the public defender sees his role not as winning the trial, but as preventing the trial from ever starting."

"Mr. Sham, this is a capital case," the judge admonished. "We should be prepared to give the public defender whatever latitude he feels he needs to give his client a fair trial."

Victor had to admire that Sham did not express disappointment at this admonishment, not even allowing himself a sigh of discontentment.

CHAPTER FIFTEEN

By the end of the first day of jury selection, only three jurors had been approved by the public defender. Victor ate dinner alone at a nearby restaurant, returned to the hotel, and called his sister with the disappointing news that the trial had not yet started and might not start for several more days.

"Stay strong," she told him.

"Yeah," he said.

All of this was done by seven o'clock. He turned on the television but merely flipped through the stations without even trying to find anything to watch. Only a minute later he switched off the television, went out on the balcony, and lit a cigarette. A cool breeze blew in off the ocean, carrying to him the cold smells of ocean salt and surf. He wondered for a moment what Colton Fischer might think about jury selection. Unfortunately—or not—he might never know. He was likely going to miss the last few classes, being here for the trial.

He finished the cigarette, went back into the hotel room, and decided to go for a walk.

When he left the hotel, he made a conscious decision to stay on the same street. His head was filled with thoughts of philosophy and trials, and he didn't want to find himself lost or turned around after dark in a strange city.

He walked along for several blocks, thinking to himself, almost talking to himself, and even gesturing to himself. Walking though he was, he was getting nowhere. What he needed, he decided, was something to take the edge off his nerves.

A few more streets down, he spotted a little bar around the corner on one of the side streets. It had a red and white sign with two letters burned out and a board nailed up over one of the windows. A narrow parking lot flanked the near side of the building, empty but for a few older cars that didn't look much better than the sign and the window of the bar. Victor decided it was perfect.

Every head in the place turned when Victor walked in the door, reminding him of when he'd had his outburst in philosophy class. This, for a change, made Victor smile. Inside the door, a long wooden bar with a brass rail extended on the right to the back wall. To the left were a couple of pool tables, with a handful of tables between and around them. Victor went down to the last stool at the bar, sat down, and ordered a beer.

The place was typical of bars Victor had seen everywhere around the world, with a few working-class drunks and a few others on their way. At the far end of the bar, two fat guys sat on stools. Even down here, Victor could hear them arguing about the relative value of various wide receivers in the football playoffs. In the middle of the bar, a skinny guy who looked to be in his fifties drooped nearly asleep over the bar, his long hair flirting with the cigarette burning in the ashtray. Two younger guys, one white and one black, played pool at the table across the bar from Victor, over by the boarded-up window. Victor chuckled to himself at this. Lou Rollins had told him once that his mother had said that whenever you see a black guy and a white guy hanging out together, it's because they're gay. Over the years, Victor and Lou had gotten a lot of laughs out of that one.

It was, Victor thought, the perfect place to check out of the world for a few hours. Within a few minutes, however, he found that this was not the case.

The problem was the guy sitting at the table nearest Victor. He was a fat white guy with a thick neck. The heavyset woman at the table with him was evidently his wife, and she seemed to be upset that he had a girlfriend. They bickered, and Victor found it difficult to ignore them.

"Why can't you be happy with just me?"

"Why can't you cook and clean?"

Victor quickly downed his beer and got another.

The couple continued to bicker.

"Why did you have to do it with *her*? She's a nasty skank."

The beer Victor liked. The arguing he did not. He tried not to look at the couple. He moved one seat down, where he could see their reflection in the mirror behind the bar. He could see the reflections of the other people, too, and wondered why the loud arguing didn't seem to bother them.

He downed the beer. The old guy tending the bar brought him another and gave him a scowl for free.

"I'm taking the baby and going back to Georgia," the woman said.

"Go ahead. While you're back there cleaning up after your drunken mother, I'll be getting more pussy here than you ever seen."

"Maybe I'll just call the cops and tell them about your little growing operation in the closet—"

Victor saw a reflected blur of movement, and the voice cut off with a gurgling sound. In the mirror, he saw the man's hand wrapped around the woman's throat, his grip so tight that his thumb was buried almost hidden into the flesh of her neck. The woman's face was already turning purple. A panicked expression swept over her, and her hands came up to his, but they were no match. The man lifted and pulled her face over the table toward his, mumbled a threat that Victor couldn't quite hear, squeezed another second, then shoved her back into her seat. The woman coughed and dipped her head. Her hair fell across her face, but Victor could tell from her posture that she was crying.

The other people in the bar continued their separate business. They had either not seen the commotion, or had chosen to ignore it.

Victor wanted to do something. Another beer had just arrived. He downed it in three swallows and ordered another. The bartender raised his eyebrows at him. Victor threw some money on the bar and lit a cigarette.

Do what? Interfere, here? Follow them home? Be the woman's babysitter? What?

The bartender brought the beer.

The couple at the table continued to talk, the woman fearful, the man patronizing, but in tones too low for Victor to catch the words.

Victor finished his beer, stubbed out his cigarette, and walked out.

―――

Halfway back to the hotel, Victor stopped in his tracks.

For the past three months, he'd been wishing every day that he could have been in a position to make a difference. Now, tonight, he was in a position to do something positive, and he had walked away.

Was he afraid of the police? No one in that bar was likely to call them.

Did he not know what should be done? Did he need a system to take care of his problems?

Without thinking about it another minute, Victor turned and walked back up the street toward the bar.

Victor got back to the parking lot just as the guy was coming out of the bar with his wife. They didn't see him coming as they went to their car, an old station wagon with wooden sides.

The woman was in the car, and the man had just closed the door on the driver's side when Victor reached it.

Victor flung the door open. The man looked up in surprise. Victor punched him square in the face, then grabbed a greasy handful of hair and pulled so that the fat man tipped partway out the door. With his other hand, Victor pulled the door closed, threatening to smash it into the fat man's face.

"You ever touch her again," Victor said, speaking through clenched teeth, "and I'll be back. You want that?"

The man struggled weakly to right himself, making no response. A thread of blood reached from his lower lip to the ground.

Victor tightened his grip on the hair and bashed him in the head with the door. "Do you?"

"No," the man said wetly. He spat blood on the ground.

Victor pushed the man back into the car, slammed the door, and walked off through the parking lot.

After a few steps, he started to run. He took the side streets. He did know the way, and he didn't get lost.

He ran all the way back to his hotel.

In the dream, he pulls the trigger and paints the back wall of the garage crimson red and gloppy white. The Iraqi man falls to the floor. He pulls the trigger again. As the Iraqi woman falls, her rifle pops out a burst of bullets. He can feel the heat, smell the gunpowder. He is amazed, again, to realize that he has not been hit. The woman flops spasmodically on the floor, bleeding profusely from her neck.

An Iraqi boy has appeared in the doorway behind the woman, eyes wide and black.

Behind him, he can hear his team scrambling for the door, rushing to get away. To be discovered here would be to jeopardize the entire mission. He knows that he goes with them, and yet, he stays here.

The Iraqi boy steps out from the doorway.

Instead of running with his team, this time he presses forward, stares hard at the boy. He stares hard into his eyes. He wants to tear apart the universe to rip the accusation from those eyes.

His mouth opens to speak, but suddenly he has no words. The rapid language instructors, he realizes suddenly, have not given him a vocabulary. The most important phrase, the one he wants desperately to say, he simply can't.

In all his language classes, they never told him the Arabic words for "I'm sorry."

In the dream, he moves close to the boy, he stares into those black eyes, and he tries with all his might to will the communication into the boy's brain.

The little boy simply stares, eyes black as infinity.

CHAPTER SIXTEEN

The following day, Victor sat through another session of jury selection. While the prosecutor and the public defender interviewed, rejected, and—very occasionally—accepted jurors, Victor sat quietly, studying Dario Mullen. He wondered if Dario had ever hit a girlfriend. He suspected he probably had, being a robbing, killing kind of guy and all. He was in deep shit now, though. This was a capital offense. If he was convicted for this, he stood a good chance of being sentenced to death. Victor wondered if the girls Dario had hit would be happy about this sentence. He suspected that they would not, and he wondered about this.

While frustrated at the pace of the proceedings, Victor was also happy that Gordon Sham had looked at the bandaged knuckles on his right hand and hadn't asked any questions. Victor had apparently cut his knuckles on the fat man's teeth, and it had been awkward enough asking the hotel desk clerk for bandages. Not too many events produced those kinds of cuts, and everyone knew what those were.

Though the progress seemed agonizingly slow, when the judge banged the gavel to adjourn the court until the next day, the prosecution and the defense had managed to select all but the last two members of the jury.

"Almost there," Victor said to Gordon Sham when everyone stood up to go.

Sham nodded. "Should be one more day of jury selection, and then the trial will begin."

Victor watched the bailiffs lead Dario Mullen out the side door of the courtroom. Almost justice.

After eating dinner alone and making the obligatory phone call to his sister, Victor thought seriously about calling Lou Rollins. What would he tell him, though? "Wish you were here?" No. "You should have been there to see the awesome jury selection?" No. "Heard any good jokes lately?" No.

What then?

How about: "You should have seen the look on that guy's face when I punched him last night!"

At one time, Victor would have been able to share a story like that with Lou. Now, though, things were different. Lou was a cop, and it was his job to arrest people for assault, not applaud them. Maybe Lou would choose to look the other way, but it would be unfair for Victor to put Lou in a position of having to make such a choice.

Out on the balcony of his hotel room again, Victor smoked a cigarette and thought about everything. He watched the moonlight twinkling on the black water as the waves rolled silently onto the beach, and it reminded him of the black water of his Mississippi. He wondered briefly when his father had last seen the Mississippi, and if the moment had carried any significance to him. When he finally threw the cigarette into the wind and went back inside, he knew he wasn't going to watch television. He'd known all along. He hadn't even taken off his shoes.

Tonight, Victor went walking the other way down the street in front of the hotel. After several blocks, he slowed down, looking for a specific kind of bar. After several more blocks, he found it across the street.

This bar occupied the end of a strip mall building. The front and side were occupied by huge windows, intact but painted black. The sign on the front showed crossed pool cues and only had one letter burned out. Victor crossed the street and walked through the parking lot to the back of the building. As he'd hoped, he found a little space behind the building, with a low wall separating it from the houses on the other side. Back there, too, Victor found a dumpster with several broken pool cues inside it.

Satisfied, excited even, he untucked his shirt, ruffled his hair, turned over part of his collar, and went inside.

Did justice require a system?

Why *couldn't* it be the action of one man?

If one man alone was all of judge, jury, and executioner, what did it matter, *if he was right?*

Inside the bar, Victor adopted a staggering shuffle, though he was stone sober. He went to the bar and got a beer, then surveyed the crowd. Although it was a weeknight, there were quite a few people in the place, and not too many drunks. Three pool tables with clean green felt sat under beer lights on the side of the room by the door. All of the tables were in use, with stacks of quarters waiting on deck. On the side of the room opposite the door, a scattering of tables sat in moderate darkness.

Victor headed over to those tables, swaying a bit as he walked.

Many of the tables had groups of guys at them. All of them noticed Victor as he made his way across the room.

Victor found a table with a half-full glass on it and sat down. A minute later a rough character wearing leather sidled up from the direction of the bathrooms. "Hey, man," he said to Victor. "You're in my seat."

"Sorry," Victor muttered meekly, then moved to an empty table down a way.

He could feel the eyes watching him. He finished his beer and took out his wallet, holding it open wide to take out a handful of bills. Money and wallet still in hand, he shuffled up to the bar for another beer. This time he got some quarters, too, from the bartender, and swayed over to the pool tables, carefully surveying the stacks of quarters already there before gingerly adding his to the farthest table.

He could feel the crowd watching him as he staggered back to his table in the darkened part of the room, bumping people and muttering apologies as he went.

Back at the table, he sat with his elbow on the table and his chin in his hand, and pretended to fall asleep.

A moment later, he jerked himself up straight and looked around as if he didn't recognize the place. Many heads were turned in his direction.

It was time.

He took one more good look through his wallet, drained the last of his beer, and headed for the door.

Outside in the cool air, he walked slowly toward the back of the parking lot. He heard the door huff open behind him, then squeak closed, but he didn't turn around to look.

Still shuffling, he went to the back alley, stumbled around the corner, and stood by the dumpster.

He had barely turned around when three thugs rounded the corner. He had seen them inside, young guys, hungry looking.

"Hey, man," one of them said. "Give us your wallet."

"Hey, man," Victor said. "Come and get it."

Ninety seconds later, Victor emerged from the back alley, tucking in his shirt and straightening his collar. Seeing the commotion had attracted no attention, he looked back at the three thugs. They were down, but they were still breathing.

"You're lucky I'm in a good mood today," he said.

As he walked back to his hotel, he wondered: was this justice?

He decided: who cares?

CHAPTER SEVENTEEN

Victor showed up at the courthouse the next day thoroughly exhausted, two hours late, and with a bruise under his left eye. As he walked in, a number of people, including most of the jury candidates, were streaming out. He located Gordon Sham in the courtroom and caught up to him as he was putting his stacks of folders and legal pads into his briefcase.

"What's going on?" Victor asked.

Sham looked at him, then focused on the bruise on Victor's face.

"I ... bumped into a wall," Victor said.

Sham shrugged. "He took the first two jurors that stood up." He nodded confidently at Victor. "Show time."

Victor felt like he should smile, but didn't. "We start tomorrow?"

Gordon Sham nodded. "Yep. First thing. Right here."

"Good," Victor said.

"Yes," Sham said, snapping his briefcase closed and looking pointedly at Victor's bandaged hand. "I'm not sure you could take much more waiting."

"Great, Victor, really great," Samantha said on the phone. He had told her about the jury selection being completed, not about the fights. "It will finally all be over."

"Yeah," Victor said.

"What about you?" she asked. "How are you holding up?"

"Oh," Victor said, and looked at his knuckles, which were scabbed over nicely now. "Fine."

Samantha was quiet on the phone. "Are you sure? You don't sound fine."

"Well, this is a tough situation, you know?"

"Yeah," Samantha said. "Have you been eating? What are you doing to stay busy there in the hotel?"

"Yes, I'm eating," he said. "And here in the hotel, I've been mostly watching television."

"Watching television?"

"Mmm-hmm."

"That doesn't sound like you."

"Yeah," he said, "but I haven't felt like myself for quite some time."

After they hung up the phone, Victor stayed in the hotel and really did watch television. Tomorrow was going to be a big day, and he didn't want to miss any of it.

Victor rose before dawn the next morning without a wake-up call, showered, dressed, and headed out. He stopped at a diner on the way to the courthouse and ordered breakfast, but was too tense to eat. He wound up simply drinking coffee and watching the clock.

The trial was set to start at eight. Victor got to the courthouse a half hour early.

Walking up to the courtroom, he found it strange that the hall was quiet. He was early, but a lot of people should have been arriving to get ready. Where was Gordon Sham? Where was Dario Mullen?

The courtroom was dark and empty. Tacked to the bulletin board outside the door was a notice. He stared at it for a moment. It was different from yesterday.

State v. Mullen—Canceled

Canceled? He looked at the paper carefully. In the margins were some codes, but none of it made any sense to him.

He spotted a bailiff passing in the hallway. "Hey." He pointed at the paper on the bulletin board. "What does this mean?"

The bailiff glanced at the paper. "It looks like the trial has been canceled."

Victor frowned. "I can see that! But, why? Did he decide to plead guilty? Does it say?"

The bailiff glanced at Victor, then squinted at the paper again and shook his head with a bit of a grimace. "No, he didn't change his plea. This says the charges were dropped."

CHAPTER EIGHTEEN

Victor found Gordon Sham in the prosecutor's office, two floors down. Gordon Sham was on the phone, but hung up as soon as he saw Victor coming in. "Victor," he said, extending his hand.

Victor ignored it. "What the fuck is going on? The trial's canceled? You dropped the charges?"

"I had to, Victor. Had to." He gestured toward the chair in front of his desk. "Please, sit down, I'll explain."

Victor didn't want to sit, and he didn't want anything explained to him. He wanted to throw something through the big window behind Sham's desk.

Sham gestured again.

With great personal effort, Victor sat down.

"Now," Gordon Sham started by saying, "let me start by saying that this thing isn't over. We're gonna have a trial, and he's gonna fry, I can guarantee you that." He paused and walked back behind his desk. "It's just not going to be today."

"What?" Victor asked. He wanted to ask something bigger, but all the air had gone out of him.

Gordon Sham sat down. "It came to my attention after you

left yesterday that Dario Mullen was not read his rights before he made his confession."

Victor stared. "So what? Is he saying now that he was coerced?"

Sham shook his head. "No, not yet, but as soon as the defense found that out, they would have challenged the confession, and if the judge threw it out, we would have had precious little."

"What? What about the witnesses?"

Sham shook his head again. "He was wearing a ski mask, and now that we don't have that, either—"

"Wait. You don't have that, either?"

Sham made a face. "Uh, that came up yesterday, too, when they were supposed to be transporting the evidence." He shook his head again. At this rate, he was going to twist his head completely off. "The police didn't fill out the tag correctly when they searched Mullen's apartment. We still have the ski mask, but now we can't show the chain of custody that brings it from his apartment to the courtroom. If we can't do that, we can't use it."

Victor said nothing, but inside he was screaming.

"Without the gun, or the mask, or the confession, I had no choice but to drop the charges immediately."

"So, it's over?"

"Oh, no, no. Not by a long shot. That's the beauty of it, you see?"

Victor didn't.

"If we went to trial now, we'd lose, and that would be it. No doubt about it. But I dropped the charges, see? Now we can go back, we can get the other evidence, we can find the gun, we can build this case back up and *then* bring it to trial."

Victor seethed. He noticed that he had his hands clenched in his lap. "How long?"

Sham looked down at his desk. "Well, that depends on a lot of things. They could find the gun right away. They're still out looking for it. Mullen could give another confession. We could find something new. Without any of that, we'll just build our case with the existing evidence—witnesses, the testimony of the girlfriend, things like that."

Victor stared at him.

"Maybe as soon as three months. Maybe as long as a year."

Victor felt like he was hollow, and filled with acid. There was nothing to do here. He stood up.

Gordon Sham stood up too and hurried around the desk. The prosecutor put his hand on Victor's wrist. It took all of Victor's will not to grab that hand and bend it back until the bones snapped and the ligaments ripped apart.

"Don't worry about this," he told Victor. "This isn't the end, not by a long shot." He took his hand off Victor's wrist, and Victor realized that he hadn't been breathing.

Back in his hotel room, Victor stood out on the balcony, smoking a cigarette, watching the waves roll up to shore, glittering diamond blue in the morning sunlight. His eyes were slanted in concentration. He was thinking about justice.

The system had failed him, but worse than that, the system had betrayed his parents.

How could justice depend on a system, when sometimes the system just didn't work?

It hadn't just failed him. Maybe it hadn't failed *him* at all. It had failed his parents, though. It had failed them in the biggest way possible.

Maybe what Gordon Sham said was true. Maybe they

would be able to get another confession, or find the gun and rebuild the case.

And maybe not, too.

Maybe the only hope his parents had for getting justice was no longer the system at all. Maybe it was him.

He threw his cigarette over the railing and watched as the wind carried it out of sight down toward the parking lot. He could smell the cold ocean mist of the waves breaking far below him. Something about the eternal ocean, always changing, but always the same, gave him some kind of stability, some kind of resolution.

He knew what he had to do, and he knew how to do it.

As he walked back into the room, a housekeeper knocked cautiously on the open door. She looked at the suitcase, which was packed but open on the bed, then at him.

"Checking out today, sir?" she asked, a fine Latin lilt in her voice.

"That's right," Victor said. "I'm going home."

CHAPTER NINETEEN

Duncan was watching out the window, and the door opened before Victor reached it. Duncan's head stuck out next to the knob. Oscar's tiny face stuck out next to Duncan's knees. Oscar growled at Victor.

"Hi, Duncan," Victor said.

"Hi, Uncle Bictor," Duncan said. He pulled his head inside the door and looked back over his shoulder. His face reappeared a moment later, lined with more worry than a three-year-old's should ever have. "My mom's crying," he said.

Victor struggled to conceal his anger. "I'm sorry," he said. "Can I come in?"

"Sure." The door swung open and Duncan stepped back. Oscar stayed close to Duncan's feet, still growling low at Victor as he entered the house. Victor smiled at him.

Samantha emerged from her bedroom, spotted Victor, and came toward him in a rush. Her eyes were puffy and red. She threw herself against Victor in a giant hug, her body shaking with sobs. He turned his face into her neck and hugged her back, trying to convey a confidence in his squeeze that he might never be able to tell her in words.

"I told them to let me tell you," Victor said to her softly. "Those bastards can't get anything right."

She sobbed harder into his chest. "I can't believe he's going to get away with it, with killing our parents."

Victor stood strong and tried to be soft and rigid at the same time. "No, he isn't."

Samantha pulled her head back and looked into Victor's eyes. "Did they call you? Did they find the gun?"

Victor shook his head. "No," he said, trying to put confidence in his voice that would penetrate her heart and shore up her soul. "I just have a feeling."

Victor had intended to stay with Samantha for only a few minutes, but he wound up staying for the better part of an hour. Samantha cried and cried, and Victor did his best to console her. All the while, Duncan stood next to his mother with his little hand on her shoulder, uncertain of what was going on but wanting to be brave like Uncle Bictor. Oscar stayed at Duncan's feet and growled at Victor every time he looked at him.

At first, he had great difficulty not telling her his plans, but he didn't want to put her in jeopardy over this. He wanted to bear this burden alone. Maybe in time he would tell her, but not now.

Presently it became time for Victor to leave, and he stood up.

"Where are you going?" Samantha asked.

"I'm going downtown to talk to Lou. I want to see if he knows anything else we can do to get this guy." It was partly true, anyway.

Samantha nodded, still in a daze. "Okay," she said. Her eyes came up to Victor's hopefully. "Do you think there's a chance?"

"Oh, yeah," Victor said, nodding grimly. "I think it's a sure thing."

She met his eyes, and finally she saw something there. Fear flashed quickly across her face, quickly replaced by a frown of determination. "Good," she said, then she said it again. "Good."

He hugged her one last time, then hugged Duncan, and left.

One down, one to go.

"That's unbelievable," Lou Rollins said. "Un-fucking-believable."

Victor said nothing.

They were back in the little jazz bar again. Victor was doing two things. First, he was filling Lou in on what had happened in Jacksonville. Second, he was establishing his presence here in St. Louis, as witnessed by an officer of the law.

Lou shook his head and continued. "Somebody better lose his job over this. We have our problems here sometimes, too, but they fucked this up bad, and on a capital murder case, no less."

Victor nodded and swallowed more of his beer.

Lou looked at him. "How are you handling this? Are you pissed?"

"Yeah, I'm pissed."

"Hmmph. Seem pretty calm to me."

Victor put his beer down. "Gordon Sham told me that they're rebuilding the case, and they'll refile the charges."

"And that's good enough for you?"

"Well, he seems to know what he's doing. Plus, what choice do I have?"

Lou snorted and shook his head. "I don't know, man, but that is some fucked up shit."

"Yeah."

They drank a few more beers before leaving. Lou promised to ask around the department and see if there was something the St. Louis police could do. Victor's parents, after all, had been residents of St. Louis. Victor let him go on about it, though he could have told him there was no need.

They left right as the band started playing, which made it too loud to talk anyway.

As Victor walked home, he almost had a spring in his step. The alibis were set. Everybody knew he was back in town.

Now it was time for phase two.

Frozen grass crunched under his feet as Victor made his way slowly across the field. When he had been here last, back in August, the lawns had been lush and green. Now they were brown and muddy. He didn't have long to spend here, but he wanted to talk to them before he left. It didn't have to make sense. He was going to do it anyway.

He found the headstones and walked up to them carefully. He had not wanted to do this. Every step—first the identification, then the funeral, now the visitation, next more visitations, then anniversaries—he didn't want to do any of it. Somewhere deep down, he felt that every step carried him farther from them, and if he could simply not take those steps, then they would stay close.

He found himself thinking about flowers. His father had been a florist. It didn't seem right that there were no flowers here, now.

Flowers. The thought swept into Victor's mind, and suddenly, his plan was complete.

He'd come here to think. He'd intended to stand here, in

whatever presence of his parents he could find, and consider his course of action. He'd wanted to think about justice, and the justice system, and what his parents would think, and about what was the right thing to do. Now, however, he didn't have time.

The idea of the flower had popped into his head unbidden, as if planted by some external entity. In this place, he could only imagine two such interested parties.

He turned on his heel and headed back to the street, back to the bus stop. Time had already been tight. With the extra stop he was going to have to make, it was all the more pressing.

There would be time for visiting later.

CHAPTER TWENTY

"How did you hear about us?" the travel agent asked. The business card she'd handed Victor said her name was Amy Bishop.

Us? thought Victor. This girl was the only one in the office, and it didn't look big enough to hold two people. "I like to support my local businesses, and I found you in the neighborhood," he said with a smile. This was only partly true. He did like to support local businesses, but the primary reason he had chosen this agency was that it was very new. He hoped the agent would be eager enough for business to not notice if he was acting a little suspiciously.

"I see," Amy said, though from the look on her face she probably didn't. "And you want a bus ticket?"

"That's right. Greyhound. Right away."

Amy looked confused.

"You can sell that, right?" Victor asked.

"Yeah, sure. It's just that, most people just go down to the station."

"Not me," Victor said. "I like to support my local businesses."

"O-kay," Amy said. She looked at him curiously. "I'm not sure I can take a credit card for this, though."

"That's all right. I want to pay cash."

Amy looked at Victor for a moment, then picked up her pen and looked down at her desk. "All right, then. I can get that for you. Can I get your name, please?"

"My name is Victor," he said, putting on a big, warm smile. "But can we not put that on the ticket? I think you can just use a password, right?"

Amy looked up from the paper at him again, this time suspicion clear in her eyes.

For a moment, Victor thought she might refuse him, though he'd already checked, and he knew his requests were perfectly within the rules. Hoping she needed the business, Victor took out his wallet and pulled out a handful of twenties, preparing to pay for the ticket.

Amy watched him fan the money out on her desk. "All right, Mr. ..."

"Storm," Victor said. He was sure now that she was on his side. "My name is Victor Storm."

"Okay, Mr. Storm, where is it you are going?"

"Jacksonville, Florida," he said, flashing her his best smile. "And please, call me Victor."

She looked at him, and her face melted into a warm smile. "Okay, Victor," she said. She pulled a thick book off a shelf beside her desk and fanned through the pages. Victor watched as her finger traced down columns of schedules, finally locating the one she was interested in. "Are you traveling for the holidays?" she asked idly.

"Not really."

"Well," she said, copying information down from the book. "If you leave tonight, you'll arrive on the twenty-first." She looked up at him with a bright smile. "First day of winter."

Victor felt his stomach tighten, and the smile left his face. He hadn't thought of this before. He didn't want a coincidence here. The last thing he needed was another link to Christmas Eve, but there was no way he could postpone things, either. This left him little room for error. "Tonight it is," he said.

Victor went back to his apartment to pick up his duffel bag, stopped at a flower shop, and was on the bus in St. Louis shortly after six o'clock. The bus left the station at six forty.

Right away, Victor felt better. He was doing something. He was on a mission.

When Victor was younger, he had taken many bus trips, and it had become his favorite mode of transportation. He loved seeing the people riding the bus, having their lives intersect with his in this random way that no one could ever have predicted. The passengers on the bus would live their entire lives, and he would live all of his, and the only time they would ever see each other was the space of a few hours on this bus, when for the briefest of moments, they shared the journey. This awed him.

Departing St. Louis, the bus crossed the river, leaving both the city of St. Louis and the state of Missouri behind. The rest of the night was a series of long highways full of headlights and small towns full of Christmas lights.

Riding through the night, Victor felt connected to his soul. On the bus, surrounded by strangers, it was easy for Victor to imagine that this was his life true life. It was easy to believe that his true life was in these nights riding on the bus, and all the other experiences—the ephemeral bustle of school and work and love and war—all of those things were merely dreams. This was easy for him to believe, and it was nice to believe.

Victor had to change buses three times: in Nashville at just after one in the morning; in Atlanta at seven in the morning; and in Lake City, Florida, at two in the afternoon. In between, there was not much time for sleep, but as the bus made its way down from Atlanta a light rain began to fall, and the steady thump of wipers and hiss of water finally lulled him to sleep.

In the dream, the Iraqi man's head explodes against the back wall, and the man falls to the ground. The woman comes out, screaming in Arabic too fast for him to understand. She is holding a rifle. People behind him shout. The rifle begins to come up. He shoots her, and she falls silent beside the man.

A boy with black hair and black eyes appears in the doorway. The boy looks at the bodies on the ground, then looks up at him. The boy's face is blank.

He steps forward, desperate to communicate something to the boy. He can't think of the words.

Suddenly he looks down at the bodies on the floor. It isn't an Iraqi man and woman anymore. The bodies have changed into an old white couple. A bloody straw hat lies next to the man's head. He bends to the bodies and turns them over.

It is his own parents, dead and bloated.

CHAPTER TWENTY-ONE

It was late afternoon when Victor stepped out from the Greyhound station in Jacksonville. The rain had stopped just this side of Lake City, and by the time he got to Jacksonville the clouds had broken up enough for the sun to shine through. Victor preferred the rain.

No rental car this time, and no taxi. He'd take the public bus to his destination. Except for that travel agent, who had probably forgotten him already and didn't know what was going on anyway, he didn't have a trail so far, and he wasn't going to start leaving one now. Buses had served him well to this point, and they would serve him well the rest of the way.

He'd picked up a local bus schedule from inside the Greyhound station. Now he took from his pocket the folded page he'd torn from the phone book back in September, looked at the map, and selected a route to 1614 Butterfield Lane.

As he rode, Victor sat with his duffel bag in his lap and watched the sun go down through the window. Inside, he felt no lament, no remorse, just cold efficiency.

The sun had set completely by the time Victor reached his destination. He got off the bus a block past the apartment complex, which turned out to be three run-down, single-story adobe buildings. The three buildings formed a *U* with the open end toward the back, a pool in the center, and a parking lot around the perimeter.

Hands in his pockets, Victor strolled casually through the complex, down one sidewalk to the back parking lot. The five apartments on this side were numbered from fourteen down to ten, and he could see that numbers nine down to six were the four across the back. That meant the one he was looking for, number two, was second from the end, back up toward the street.

Looking around the darkness of the back parking lot, Victor found he was alone. He ducked between two cars, opened his duffel bag, and got ready, which meant pulling on his black leather gloves, unwrapping the handgun he'd prepared specially for the occasion, and tucking it into his belt.

Victor had always enjoyed riding the bus on long trips, but one advantage of taking the bus for this trip was that his baggage did not have to go through metal detectors.

A glance around the parking lot told him he was still alone. Hiking his duffel bag up onto his left shoulder, he put the gun in his right hand, and his hand inside the open front of his jacket. All set.

Alert for any trouble, he walked slowly, deliberately, down the sidewalk past the apartments.

Five ... four ... three ... two.

As he passed the window toward the door to number two, his heart froze in his chest. The Venetian blinds in the window were slanted down toward the inside, but not quite closed all the way.

Inside, next to the dingy little Christmas tree, a small boy with bright blond hair was playing with a wooden train.

Victor passed the door to number two and kept on walking, out of the complex and all the way across the street.

CHAPTER TWENTY-TWO

On the covered sidewalk in front of a strip mall across the street from Dario Mullen's apartment, Victor paced back and forth in front of a health food supplement store, his mind racing.

He'd come all this way to avenge his parents' murder, and now he could not do it.

He hadn't seen this coming, hadn't planned on it at all. Gordon Sham had never mentioned that Dario Mullen had a son. No one had ever mentioned the possibility. Dario was unmarried, unemployed, a dead-end guy in a dead-end city in a dead-end world. What the fuck was he doing with a son?

All at once, Victor turned and frowned at the apartment complex across the street. Was it possible that the kid was not his son? Was it possible that this was someone else's kid, maybe a neighbor's kid that he was babysitting, or something like that?

No. Dario Mullen had murdered two people in cold blood. The police had thus far botched the case, but everybody knew it. No mother was going to let a guy like that watch her kid, no matter how hard-up for a babysitter.

So, what was he going to do?

Could he let Gordon Sham rebuild his case, give that a try first? Could he just turn around and go home now, and just hope that Sham and his team were able to come up with some evidence to reinstate the charges? He didn't think so.

Could he put his demons aside and just go back over there and shoot Dario, not caring whether his kid saw or not? Maybe that would be a good lesson for the kid: this is what happens if you kill people. Good lesson or not, could Victor live with himself afterward? He didn't think he could do that, either.

Maybe there was something else he could do, some choice between one or the other.

Maybe. Like what?

Well, maybe he could stake out the place for a few days, learn Dario's routine. Maybe the kid wasn't with him all the time, or maybe Victor could come up with some plan to separate the two. The big problem with this idea was that Christmas Eve would be here in a few days. Even if Victor could confront those demons, Samantha would notice if he wasn't around for the holidays. That would not do.

After twenty minutes he was still pacing back and forth in the darkness in front of the supplement store. He was so absorbed in his thoughts that he almost didn't notice when the beat-up sedan pulled into the parking lot and parked close to apartment two.

He did notice, though, and he stopped pacing and leaned against one of the wooden posts that supported the overhang.

Someone—it looked like a man—waited in the car. Smoke coming out the tailpipe into the cool air indicated the engine was still running. Someone else—clearly a woman—got out of the car. She walked briskly, with her hands in her coat pockets, around the front corner of the building and straight to the door of apartment number two. Her hand came out of her pocket, and she knocked at the door. Light slanted out onto the sidewalk as the front door opened, and even across the street Victor could hear the little boy shout, "Mommy!"

She didn't go inside. She waited a moment in the doorway, her body language indicating she was not happy to be there, and presently the little boy returned, now wearing his coat and carrying a large paper bag. The woman took the little boy back around the corner to the car. The light from Dario Mullen's front door vanished. The car pulled to the end of the driveway, then turned up the street in front of Victor, back in the direction Victor had come on the bus. The headlights flashed briefly across Victor as the car turned past him. He watched the taillights recede and finally disappear in the distance.

The anguish in Victor's heart was replaced at once by something resembling happiness, then soon after with nothing but cold. He waited for a few more minutes in the darkness, long enough to make sure the car wasn't coming right back, but short enough that Dario Mullen wouldn't go anywhere himself. Then it was time.

Victor made sure he was ready, crossed the street, and knocked lightly on the door of apartment two.

The door swung open almost at once. Dario Mullen was wearing a sleeveless T-shirt and jeans.

Victor took his hand out of his jacket and pointed the barrel of the gun at Dario's eye. "Hi, asshole," he said. "Remember me?"

CHAPTER TWENTY-THREE

Dario cowered away, spluttering, and his hands went up in front of his face. "What the fuck! Geesh!"

Victor stepped inside, closed the door, and dropped his duffel bag, all without ever taking his eyes, or the gun, off Dario. "Do you know who I am?"

Dario was still backing away with his hands up in front of his face. "No."

"Look!" Victor ordered.

Dario bumped into the dining table between the living room with the dirty blue shag carpet and the kitchen with the yellow linoleum. He dropped his hands enough to peek at Victor, and his eyes widened. He turned his face away. "You're that guy from the court."

"That's right," Victor said. "You killed my parents."

"Those charges were dropped!" Dario shouted.

Victor stayed calm. He even lowered the gun a bit. "That's what I'm here to talk to you about."

Dario blinked at him.

Victor lowered the gun a bit more. "Can we talk a minute, Dario?"

Dario lowered his hands a little, frowning, confused.

"That's right," Victor said. "I just want to talk to you." Around the dining table were three tubular steel chairs with wicker seats and backs, all more or less straight and intact. Victor waved the gun in the direction of the chairs and started, slowly, across the room. "Go ahead, sit down."

Dario looked uncertain, but he seemed to decide that sitting at the table and talking was better than getting shot in the face, so he pulled out the chair on the far side of the table and gingerly sat down.

Victor approached slowly and pulled out the seat opposite Dario. Slowly, very slowly, he sat down in the chair and laid the gun down on the table. He forced a wicked little smile. "Isn't this better?"

Dario grunted.

"Now, as I was saying," Victor said, "you killed my parents because they got in the way of you getting a little cash."

"Those char—"

Victor held up a hand. "I know, I know. Those charges were dropped. But did you know that they plan to refile those charges?"

Dario frowned at him.

"It's true," Victor said. "They're working right now to put together the witnesses, and the evidence, and the DNA." Victor just threw that in there. "They're building up an airtight case against you, and then they're going to reinstate the charges."

Dario looked concerned. "They can't do that."

"Oh, yes, they can, Dario," Victor said, letting a little gloat into his voice. Inside, he wondered briefly if the public defender had not told him of this possibility. Maybe, once the charges were dropped, the public defender was no longer representing him, and therefore had no obligation to tell him.

Dario frowned at the table and shifted in his seat.

Victor leaned forward. His hand was still on the gun, but now he was speaking as if they were co-conspirators. "You know what's going to happen then, Dario?"

Dario didn't.

"They're going to find you guilty, Dario, and they're going to sentence you to death. You're going to fry."

Florida did not use an electric chair, or any other frying devices, for its executions, but this did not stop Dario from wincing. "It was an accident," he said. "I didn't mean to do it."

Victor remembered identifying the bodies. His father had a hole right above his eyebrow. His mother had been shot in the back. "I know it was, Dario," he said calmly. "I know it was. That's why I'm here to offer you a way out."

An expression of hope flickered briefly over Dario's face, then his eyes returned to the gun. "What way out?"

Victor pushed the gun across the table to him. "I'm going to let you kill yourself."

Dario's eyes stayed on the gun, now in the center of the table. "Kill myself?"

Victor drew his hands back and put them in his lap. "That's right."

"I don't think I want to do that."

Victor raised an eyebrow at him. "You'd rather let the state do it for you? You'd rather squirm in pain than get it over with now, quick and easy?"

Dario shifted in his seat, his eyes still on the gun. He was starting to breathe quicker. "Maybe they won't do that. Maybe they won't find more evidence."

"Oh, yes, they will," Victor said, feigning great confidence. "I spoke to the prosecutor earlier today, and he told me they were almost ready now."

Now Dario's eyes came up to Victor's, searching. "He did?"

Victor nodded.

"But, I have a kid," Dario protested.

"And that's precisely why you should do it," Victor said, energy rising in his voice. "What do you want your son to think about his father? That he let the state tie him down and kill him like a dog? Or that he went out on his own terms, when *he* wanted to, the man's way out?"

Dario's eyes went back to the gun in the center of the table. "I guess I really don't have any choice, then, do I?"

"Not the way I see it."

Dario fell silent. A glazed and sad look came into his eyes.

"Do it, Dario," Victor urged. "Pick up the gun, and do it."

Dario reached over the table and hefted the gun in his right hand.

"Do it," Victor hissed.

Dario held the gun up in front of his face, blinking at the black metal.

"Do it!"

Suddenly, the sad look left Dario's face. A strange focus came into his dark eyes. He looked from the gun to Victor. "I don't think so," he said. "I think I'll shoot you instead."

In a blink, he whipped the gun around at Victor's head and pulled the trigger.

The gun inches from his face, so close he could smell the gunmetal and cleaning oil, Victor smiled. Now, he was certain.

There was a metallic click.

Dario's eyes widened in surprise.

In a blur of movement, Victor ripped the gun from Dario's hand. "I was afraid of that," he said, still smiling grimly. He turned the gun around in his right hand. His thumb pressed a button, and the empty magazine dropped to the floor.

Victor's other hand came up from under the table. The magazine gleamed wickedly in the overhead light until it disappeared into the butt of the gun and clicked into place. Victor pulled the slide back and let it snap forward, locking a bullet into the chamber.

"No!" Dario realized what was going on and jumped in his chair, trying to get away.

Victor put the gun to his head and pulled the trigger.

This time, the gun did not click. This time, it popped.

A cone of crimson sprayed the wall, the phone, the refrigerator.

It was everything Victor could do not to shoot twice, not to empty the magazine into the scum's skull. Instead, he put things in place—gun dropped from Mullen's hand, flower from his duffel bag on the table—and walked out.

CHAPTER TWENTY-FOUR

Twenty-four hours later, Victor walked up the steps to Samantha's townhouse. This time again she yanked the door open before he reached it and met him on the stoop. Her expression was blank, as if she had run out of emotion.

"I just got a call from Gordon Sham," she said.

Victor's heart went dizzy light, but he kept his face blank. "Yes?"

Samantha threw her arms around his neck. "Dario Mullen killed himself."

Victor hugged her back, hard, and said nothing.

Two little faces peeked at them from the door. Duncan grinned at him. Oscar growled.

Gordon Sham picked up the phone on the first ring.

"Dario Mullen killed himself?" Victor asked.

"It appears so."

"Appears?"

"Well, these things are never certain until the investigation is officially complete, but right now—his fingerprints were the only ones on the gun, and no one saw anyone enter or leave the apartment between the time his girlfriend picked up their kid last night and the time the apartment manager stopped in to check in on him this morning."

"Was the gun …?"

"I know what you're thinking, but no, it's the wrong caliber to be the one he used to kill your parents." Sham chuckled a bit into the phone. "He had it around for mischievous purposes, though."

"Really?"

"Positively. The gun had the serial number filed off it. You only do that if you're going to use the gun for a crime."

"Yeah, that seems likely." Though he was on the phone, Victor still suppressed a smile. "So, you're sure it was suicide, then? I mean, it wasn't accidental. He did it on purpose?"

"Well, like I said, the investigation isn't officially closed, but I'm sure it will be soon. The possibility of an accident or something else hasn't been ruled out yet, but there was one thing at the scene that seems to indicate he was thinking about what he'd done to your parents, and he just couldn't handle it."

"What's that?"

"Your father was a florist, right?"

"Yes."

"Well, when Dario Mullen left his brains against the back wall, he left a black carnation on the table."

This time, Victor didn't even try to suppress his smile.

"Killed himself?" Lou Rollins said, then grunted. "That's pretty unusual."

Victor raised his eyebrows. "It is?"

Lou looked at him steadily. "Most people that kill themselves over a murder, it's because they killed someone they loved and they can't live with the guilt."

"Really?"

"Uh-huh. I don't know if I've ever heard of someone feeling so remorseful over killing strangers."

Victor shrugged. "Maybe Dario had a deep and caring soul."

Lou looked hard at Victor. "Maybe." He took a drink from his beer, set it down on the table, and rolled the glass between his palms. "Too bad there won't be a trial, though."

The waitress arrived with a plate of chicken wings and a fresh beer for Victor.

"Why's that?" Victor asked.

"For you," Lou said. "People just like hearing the word *guilty*. It does something for them."

Victor picked up a chicken wing and bit off a chunk. "I'll be all right. Justice was served."

Lou thought about this and seemed to relax a bit. He picked up a chicken wing. "You think that's what it was—justice?" he asked.

"Yes, I do."

"Even without the trial?"

Victor smiled. "Haven't you heard, Lou? Justice is a philosophical concept. The justice system is a bureaucracy of men for the enforcement—"

"Yeah, I heard."

"Well," Victor said. "Dario got justice."

Lou nodded thoughtfully. "To tell the truth, though, Victor, I was afraid you were going to go down there, take care of Dario yourself."

"You were, huh?" Victor kept his eyes steady. "What did you think about that?"

Lou munched a chicken wing, then pointed the bone at Victor. "I thought it would serve the bastard right."

———

In the dream, he is a kid on a fall day. He is hit with a rock, and is chased into a garage. He knows he is dreaming, but he can't wake up.

He is a young soldier in the Special Forces, his team is discovered, and he kills a man and a woman. Sometimes, after he has killed them, the Iraqi man and woman become his own parents, dead and bloated. He knows he is dreaming, but he can't wake up.

A young child with black hair and black eyes emerges from the doorway. He looks at the bodies, then looks up at him. His face is blank, but his eyes are black as infinity, black as the end of the barrel of a gun.

Sometimes the child has blond hair, and sometimes he carries a wooden toy train, but always his face is blank, and his eyes are as black as justice.

He knows he is dreaming, but he can't wake up.

———

The thud of the Sunday newspaper against the front door of Victor's parents' condominium snapped his eyes open. The threads of a familiar dream fell away from his brain. His heart was racing and his sheets were soaked. He pushed the blankets off himself to the side, then sat up and swung his feet down to the floor.

The vertical blinds were open, and far out to the east he

could see the first touches of light beginning to trace the distant horizon. The condominium was silent and dark. Pulling a robe around himself, he slid the Arcadia door open and walked out onto the balcony. The crisp winter air pricked his skin.

The Mississippi River wound across in front of him. To the right he could see the Arch, rising and falling like hopes and dreams. He looked down toward the ground. Nine floors. How easy it would be to slip over the railing, to fall.

Truth, war, justice—all of it would just ... fall away.

A tiny breeze chilled the hair behind his ears and on his wrists.

It would be so easy.

After a long time, Victor turned back into the condominium, went to the front door, and got the newspaper.

ABOUT THE AUTHOR

Born and raised in upstate New York, Terry F. Torrey has spent most of his adult life in Arizona with his amazing wife, awesome daughter, and remarkable cats. A lifelong learner, he was most pleased to complete the acclaimed Creative Writing program at Phoenix College.

Terry F. Torrey writes an eclectic variety of quirky, compelling, and heartfelt books and shorts, including campy but realistic pop-culture monster novels, page-turning vigilante action novels, riveting suspense novels with shades of noir, cozy upstate campus mysteries, clean contemporary westerns, and sharp works of political satire.

Find all of Terry F. Torrey's writings at terryftorrey.com.

Made in the USA
Columbia, SC
19 April 2024